# Resolution

# Resolution

## ROBERT B. PARKER

G. P. PUTNAM'S SONS

*New York*

PUTNAM

G. P. PUTNAM'S SONS
*Publishers Since 1838*
Published by the Penguin Group
Penguin Group (USA) Inc., 375 Hudson Street, New York, New York 10014, USA •
Penguin Group (Canada), 90 Eglinton Avenue East, Suite 700, Toronto, Ontario
M4P 2Y3, Canada (a division of Pearson Canada Inc.) • Penguin Books Ltd, 80
Strand, London WC2R 0RL, England • Penguin Ireland, 25 St Stephen's Green,
Dublin 2, Ireland (a division of Penguin Books Ltd) • Penguin Group (Australia),
250 Camberwell Road, Camberwell, Victoria 3124, Australia (a division of Pearson
Australia Group Pty Ltd) • Penguin Group India Pvt Ltd, 11 Community Centre,
Panchsheel Park, New Delhi–110 017, India • Penguin Group (NZ), 67 Apollo
Drive, Rosedale, North Shore 0632, New Zealand (a division of Pearson New
Zealand Ltd) • Penguin Books (South Africa) (Pty) Ltd, 24 Sturdee Avenue,
Rosebank, Johannesburg 2196, South Africa

Penguin Books Ltd, Registered Offices:
80 Strand, London WC2R 0RL, England

Library of Congress Cataloging-in-Publication Data

Parker, Robert B., date.
Resolution / Robert B. Parker.
p.    cm.
ISBN-13: 978-0-399-15504-8
1. Title.
PS3566.A686R47      2008                    2008006589
813'.54—dc22

Printed in the United States of America
1   3   5   7   9   10   8   6   4   2

BOOK DESIGN BY AMANDA DEWEY

This is a work of fiction. Names, characters, places, and incidents either are the product
of the author's imagination or are used fictitiously, and any resemblance to actual per-
sons, living or dead, businesses, companies, events, or locales is entirely coincidental.

While the author has made every effort to provide accurate telephone numbers and
Internet addresses at the time of publication, neither the publisher nor the author as-
sumes any responsibility for errors, or for changes that occur after publication. Further,
the publisher does not have any control over and does not assume any responsibility for
author or third-party websites or their content.

*As always, for Joan, the girl of the golden west . . .*
*and east . . . and north . . . and south*

# Resolution

# 1.

I was in the Blackfoot Saloon in a town called Resolution, talking with the man who owned the saloon about a job. The owner was wearing a brocade vest. His name was Wolfson. He was tall and thin and sort of spooky-looking, with a walleye.

"What's your name?" Wolfson said.

"Hitch," I said. "Everett Hitch."

"How long you been in Resolution?" Wolfson said.

We were at the far end of the big mahogany bar, sipping whiskey that I had bought us.

"'Bout two hours," I said.

"And you come straight here?" Wolfson said.

"Ain't that many choices in Resolution," I said.

"There's some others," Wolfson said. "But they ain't as nice. Tell me about yourself. What can you do?"

"Went to West Point," I said. "Soldiered awhile, scouted awhile, shotgun for Wells Fargo, did some marshaling with Virgil Cole."

"Cole?"

"Yep."

"You worked with Virgil Cole?" Wolfson said. "Where?"

"Lotta towns, last one was Appaloosa."

"And you were doing gun work," Wolfson said.

"Some."

"Virgil Cole," Wolfson said.

I nodded and sipped some of the whiskey.

"We got no marshal in this town," Wolfson said. "Sheriff's deputy rides over once in a while from Liberty. But mostly we're on our own."

I nodded.

"Got a mayor?" I said. "Town council? Anything like that?"

"Nope."

"Who's in charge?"

"In town? Nobody. In here? Me," Wolfson said.

I glanced around the saloon. It was half full in the middle of the afternoon. Nobody looked dangerous. The lookout chair at the other end of the bar was empty. I nodded at it.

"Could use a lookout," Wolfson said. "Last one got hoorahed out of town."

"What are you paying?" I said.

He told me.

"Plus a room upstairs," Wolfson said.

"Meals?"

"If you eat them here," Wolfson said.

"Anyplace else in town to eat?" I said.

Wolfson shrugged.

"I'll take it," I said.

"It's kind of a tradition," Wolfson said. "Some of the boys like to test the new lookout."

I nodded.

"Fact is I've had trouble keeping a lookout."

I nodded again, and drank a little more. The whiskey was pretty good.

"I got a big capital investment here," Wolfson said. "I don't want it wrecked."

"Don't blame you," I said.

"Think you can stick?" Wolfson said.

"Sure," I said.

"Some tough people here," Wolfson said.

"Tough people everywhere," I said.

"Any chance you could get Virgil Cole to come up here, too?" Wolfson said.

"No," I said.

"You fellas on the outs?" Wolfson said.

"No," I said.

"There's a shotgun behind the bar," Wolfson said.

"Got my own," I said.

"When you want to start?"

"Tonight," I said. "Gimme time to stow my gear, clean up, take a nap."

"It can get rough," Wolfson said.

"Any backup?" I said. "Bartenders?"

Wolfson shook his head.

"They serve drinks," Wolfson said. "Ain't got no interest in getting killed."

"You?" I said.

"I'm a businessman," Wolfson said.

"You're heeled," I said.

Wolfson opened his coat and showed me a Colt in a shoulder holster.

"Self-defense," he said. "Only."

"So I'm on my own," I said.

Wolfson nodded.

"Still interested?" he said.

"Oh, yeah," I said. "Sure. Just getting the way it lays out."

"And you ain't scared," Wolfson said.

"Not yet," I said.

# 2.

I had an eight-gauge shotgun that I'd taken with me when I left Wells Fargo. It didn't take too long for things to develop. I sat in the tall lookout chair in the back of the saloon with the shotgun in my lap for two peaceful nights. On my third night it was different.

I could almost smell trouble beginning to cook as people came into the saloon after work. There were more than usual of them and they seemed sort of excited and expectant. In addition to trouble, the saloon smelled of coal oil, and sweat, and booze, and tobacco, and food cooking, and the loud perfume of the whores. There were six men who had arrived early, sitting at a table near me, drinking whiskey. The trouble would come from them. And it would start with a sort of weaselly-looking fella in a bowler hat, wearing a gun. Everyone at the table was looking at me, and around the room, trying to look nonchalant, the rest of the customers had situated themselves where they could watch.

"Hey Lookout," the Weasel said. "What's your name?"

"Hitch," I said. "Everett Hitch."

He was wearing a dark shirt with vertical stripes, buttoned up tight at the collar. The buttons were big.

"Any good with that shotgun?" the Weasel said.

The room was quiet now, and everyone was watching. The Weasel liked that. He lounged back a little in his chair, his bowler hat tipped forward over his forehead. The gun he carried was a Colt, probably a .44, probably single-action. He had cut the holster down for a fast draw. And wore it tied to his thigh. Probably the local gunny.

"Don't need to be all that good with a double-barreled eight-gauge," I said.

"And I bet you ain't," the Weasel said.

"Wouldn't make much difference to you," I said.

"Why's that?" the Weasel said.

"I was to give you both barrels, from here," I said, "blow your head off and part of your upper body."

"You think," the Weasel said.

He was enjoying this less.

"Yep, probably kill some folks near you, too," I said. "With the scatter."

I cocked both barrels. The sound of them cocking was very loud in the room. Virgil Cole always used to say, *You gotta kill someone, do it quick. Don't look like you got pushed into it. Look like you couldn't wait to do it.* It was as if I could hear his voice as I looked at the men in front of me: *Sometimes you got to kill one person early, to save killing four or five later.*

I leveled the shotgun straight at the Weasel.

"Hey," he said, his voice much softer than it had been. "What the hell are you doing. I ain't looking for trouble. None of us looking for trouble, are we, boys?"

Nobody at the table was looking for trouble.

"I'll be damned," I said. "I thought you were."

"No, no," the Weasel said. "Just getting to know you."

He finished his drink and stood.

"Gonna drift," he said. "See how loose things are down the street."

I nodded.

"See you again, Hitch," the Weasel said.

"I imagine you will," I said.

The Weasel sauntered out, followed, maybe less jauntily, by the rest of his party. The silence hung for a minute in the room, the sounds of the saloon reemerged. Wolfson came down the bar and stopped by my chair.

"That went well," he said.

I nodded.

"Who's he?" I said.

"Name's Wickman, works for O'Malley out at the mine."

"He's not a miner," I said.

"No, gun hand. Got kind of a reputation around here," Wolfson said. "He won't like that you backed him down."

"Don't blame him," I said.

"He'll likely come at you again," Wolfson said.

"Likely," I said.

"What'll you do then?" Wolfson said.

"Kill him," I said.

# 3.

In the saloon kitchen, the Chinaman made me biscuits and fried sowbelly for breakfast. I had two cups of coffee with it, and drank the second one on the front porch of the saloon. The sun was coming up behind me, and the weather was clear. I could see most of Resolution from where I stood. It was a raw town. Newer than Appaloosa, raw lumber, mostly unpainted, boards warping as they dried. Flat-front, mostly one-story buildings, with long, low front porches, covered by a roof. The saloons generally had second floors. And sometimes a second-floor porch.

I finished the coffee and put the cup down and strolled Main Street. There were three saloons besides the Blackfoot. There was an unpainted one-story shack with a sign in the front window that read *Genuine Chicago Cooking.* There were no customers yet. A Chinaman with a long pigtail was outside, sweeping down the porch. He kept his head down as I passed. I stopped in to the livery stable to visit my horse. There was a bucket of water in his stall, and some oats in another bucket. He seemed sort of glad to see me. He nudged at my shoulder and I gave him a piece of sugar that I'd taken from the saloon.

Past the livery stable were a couple of independent whorehouses where the girls lived and worked. No gambling, no food, just short sessions for a dollar. No one appeared to be awake in the whorehouses yet. Beyond, a little away from the wooden buildings, were a few tents where the Chinamen lived, maybe ten to a tent. They cooked in the saloons, and washed floors, and washed dishes, and emptied spittoons and chamber pots and slop buckets. They laundered clothes, and ironed and sewed. They mucked out the livery stables. And I knew they stepped aside when any white man encountered them in the street. I had heard someplace that they sent all their money back to China and lived on a few pennies a month.

Where I was standing, the main street petered out into a trail that led slowly downhill toward the south. Out a ways on the trail was a small ranch. Homesteader, probably. Beyond that further out, another one, and on the horizon, a couple more. I looked at the plains for a while, stretching out wide and, to my eye, empty, to the horizon. Behind me, Main Street stretched the length of the ugly little town. At the north end it became a two-wagon rut road that went up into the hills and wound out of sight among the bull pines.

I walked back along the main street. The sun was above

the low buildings now and shone hard on me from the right. I passed the Blackfoot Saloon. It was the largest building in town. Besides the saloon, there was the hotel, the hotel dining room, a small bank, and the big general store. Past the Blackfoot was a blacksmith shop. The smith was there in his undershirt, loading charcoal into his forge. We nodded as I passed him.

I reached the north end of the main street. I looked at the pines. There were bird sounds, and the rustle of a light and occasional wind in the trees. Nothing else moved. The walk the length of the town had taken maybe ten minutes. Town was pretty small. Lotta space around it.

A whore I knew back in Appaloosa had asked me once if I got lonely, moving around in all this empty space, stopping in little towns with nothing much there. I told her I didn't. I'm not hard to get along with, but I'm not convivial. I like my own company, and I like space.

A bullet clipped one of the pine trees' branches five feet to my right. The sound of the shot was behind me. I drew, spun, and went flat on the ground. Nothing moved in the town. I waited. No second shot. After a time I stood and holstered my Colt. I walked back to the blacksmith shop.

"Hear a gunshot?" I said.

"Yep," he said. "I did."

"Know where it came from?" I said.

"Nope. You?"

"Nope," I said.

We both stood and looked musingly back along the street toward where I had been standing.

"There's a fella, name of Wickman," I said. "Kind of sharp face, little eyes. Wears one of them round bowler hats. Carries a gun in a fast-draw rig."

"Koy Wickman," the smith said. "You think he shot at you?"

"Just speculatin'," I said. "Seen him around this morning?"

"Nope. It was Koy shot at you, though, he wouldn'ta missed."

"'Less he was bein' playful," I said.

"You need to walk sorta careful around Koy Wickman," the blacksmith said. "He's pretty quick."

"I'll be sorta careful," I said.

And I was. I walked sort of careful the rest of the way back to the Blackfoot.

# 4.

I was sitting lookout, with the shotgun in my lap. Wolfson was sipping whiskey and leaning on the wall next
to my chair.

"Northwest of town," he said, "there's a big lumbering
operation. Fella named Fritz Stark. Other side of the hill,
on the east slope, is the O'Malley mine. Eamon O'Malley.
Open-pit copper mining. There's a rail spur shuttles through
the valley, back of the hill. Picks up lumber from Fritzie
Stark, copper from Eamon, and heads on east to the main
line at Mandan junction."

"Wickman works for the copper mine," I said.

"Yep."

"Why does a copper mine need a gunny?" I said. "Or is
it just a hobby?"

Wolfson sampled his whiskey, rolled it over his tongue a little, nodded approval to himself.

"Pretty good," he said. "Got it from a new drummer."

He sampled it again.

"Koy Wickman's a real gun hand," he said. "Good at it, likes it. Most folks in Resolution walk around him pretty light."

"What's he do for the mine?" I said.

"I think mostly he walks around with Eamon, intimidates folks."

"Eamon need that?"

"I don't know, exactly," Wolfson said.

All the time we talked, Wolfson surveyed the saloon. It was kind of hard to see what he was looking at, because of the walleye.

"This is a new town," Wolfson said. "We're sort of just starting to figure out what we want to do here, you know?"

"And who'll be in charge of doing it?" I said.

"Well, it ain't come to that yet," Wolfson said. "But you got the mine, you got the lumber company, you got us here in town, and you got a few sodbusters out in the flats below town."

I nodded.

"They much trouble?" I said.

"Nope, ain't that many of them," Wolfson said. "Yet."

"Other lookouts," I said. "Wickman involved in running them off?"

"Yes," Wolfson said. "Killed one of them."

"Which you didn't mention when you hired me," I said.

Wolfson shrugged.

"Figured you might not take the job," he said.

"Guys like Wickman weren't around, there wouldn't be work for guys like me," I said.

"So you gonna stick?" Wolfson said.

"Sure," I said. "But I may have to kill him in your saloon."

"You think he'll keep pushing?" Wolfson said.

"I think he needs to be the only rooster in the barnyard," I said. "Or his boss does."

Wolfson continued to look around the room for a time.

Then he said, "It's a nice business I'm growing here. The store, the hotel, the restaurant, the saloon. Nice business."

I didn't say anything.

"Can't keep hiring lookouts," he said.

I nodded. He looked around some more.

"You do what you gotta do," he said.

# 5.

Wickman came in late in the evening, wearing his fast-draw rig and his bowler hat. The hat was tipped down over his forehead.

"Hey," he said, "Hitch. I heard you was up the north end of town this morning, looking at the pine trees."

I looked straight at him and didn't say anything.

"Heard somebody took a shot at your ass," he said.

I kept looking.

"I was you I might not go walking around," he said. "You know? I might stay right here in the saloon and hide behind my shotgun."

*Go right at 'em,* Virgil used to say. *There's trouble, go right at 'em. Right now.*

"You shoot at me?" I said.

"Me," Wickman said.

He was playing to the audience that had begun to gather.

"Me?" he said. "Why would you think it was me?"

"'Cause you're a back shooter," I said.

The banter went out of Wickman's voice.

"I ain't no back shooter," he said. "You don't know nothing about me. Every man I killed was facing me straight up."

"I know a back shooter when I see one," I said. "I bet you never shot a man wasn't drunk. This morning you missed me by five feet."

"I missed shit," Wickman said. "I wanted to I coulda put that bullet right between your ears."

"So you was just thinking to scare me," I said.

Wickman opened his mouth and closed it and backed away a step.

"Didn't work," I said.

"I'm just saying it was me shot at you I wouldn'ta missed."

"Naw," I said. "'Course you wouldn't. You'da drilled me from behind, back shooter."

"Don't call me that," Wickman said.

The audience began to spread out a little. I thumbed back both hammers on the shotgun and rested the butt on my thigh with the barrels pointing at the ceiling.

"You ain't behind me now," I said.

"You think I'm going up against that eight-gauge," Wickman said.

"I ain't pointing it at you," I said.

The audience spread out farther.

"I'm pointing the shotgun at the ceiling," I said. "Good gun hand should be able to clear leather and drill me 'fore I can drop the barrels."

I was right, there were people who could win that matchup, and I wouldn't have made them the offer. But I was betting that Koy Wickman wasn't one of them. I was probably the first person he went up against that he couldn't bully, maybe the first one that was sober, and almost certainly the first one that was sober and had an eight-gauge shotgun. He backed up another step. The audience gave him plenty of room.

"Want go drink a little courage," I said. "Come back later?"

He went for it. He was pressured, probably scared, and I was right. He wasn't that good. He fumbled the draw slightly and I hit him in the face with both barrels. It turned him completely around and propelled him about three steps before he went down. It didn't blow his head off like I'd said it would. But it was an awful mess. I reloaded.

The room echoed with silence, the way it usually did after a shooting. The smell of my gunshots was strong. Wickman's Colt was ten feet from his outstretched hand. He'd never even aimed it. People looked briefly at what was left of Wickman and looked quickly away. The people who had been standing closest to him were spattered with blood and tissue. One man took his stained shirt off and threw it away from him. I thought about Virgil Cole again.

*You gotta kill someone, do it quick. Don't look like you got*

*pushed into it. Look like you couldn't wait to do it. . . . Sometimes*
*you got to kill one person early, to save killing four or five later.*

Wolfson came into the saloon from wherever he'd been, with two Chinamen. One Chinaman had a big piece of canvas, the other one had a bucket and mop. He nodded at the mess I'd made on his floor.

"You fix," he said to the two Chinamen. "You clean one time. Chop, chop."

The men went about it without expression. The one with the tarp wrapped it around Wickman and dragged him out through the door they'd come in. The other one mopped the floor.

"Anyone comes down from Liberty to ask about this," Wolfson said, "I'll talk to them. Everybody saw him draw on you . . . and the sheriff's a friend of mine."

I nodded, thinking still about Virgil's advice. Virgil was always clear, and he was always certain. But he wasn't always right.

I was hoping he would be, this time.

# 6.

Koy Wickman had been the toughest man in town, and I had killed him. It appeared that now I was the toughest man in town. And it made for a highly increased level of civility in the Blackfoot Saloon. I waited to hear from the O'Malley Mining Company. But nothing was forthcoming. Meanwhile, I sat in my high chair each evening amid the pleasant hubbub of a successful saloon. Days I read some, and rode my horse around, looking at the country. It was pretty unstressful, and I didn't mind it for a while. Sooner or later, I knew it would get boring, and I would have to move on. But for now it was good to sort of rest up from my days with Virgil in Appaloosa.

It was a Tuesday night when things began to change a bit. I was in my chair when a little whore named Billie came into the saloon, walking fast, and headed for me. Billie always claimed to be twenty, but she looked to me about fifteen. And this night she also looked scared.

"There's a man gonna get me, Everett," she said.

"Customer?" I said.

"Yes," Billie said. "But he don't want to just fuck me. He wants to do things to me, you know?"

"Hurtful things?" I said.

"Yes," she said. "I don't have to let him do hurtful things, do I, Everett?"

"No," I said.

A squat, bowlegged fella with long arms came through the same door Billie had entered and looked around the room. He spotted Billie and came toward her hard, pushing people out of the way. He didn't appear to be heeled, but I could see the handle of a knife sticking out of the top of his right boot. Billie saw him and hunched up behind my chair.

"Everett," she said.

I nodded.

"Be all right, Billie, just stay quiet."

Again she said, "Everett."

Again I nodded. The man with the knife in his boot shoved a drinker aside to get next to Billie, who had wedged herself behind my chair. He grabbed her arm.

"Everett," Billie said.

"Let her go," I said to the knife man.

"I want that whore," he said.

"Make the usual arrangements," I said. "But no grabbing."

He took his hand off her arm. I was pretty sure he knew I was the guy who killed Koy Wickman. On the other hand, he was drunk, and drunks can be stupid.

"I already paid for the little bitch," he said.

"And you already done business?" I said.

"I fucked him," Billie said.

"So?" I said to the guy with the knife.

"So she run off 'fore I was through."

"He wanted to do stuff that hurt," Billie said.

"I paid for her," he said to me.

"That's for fucking," I said. "It don't cover hurting."

"I wasn't gonna hurt her," he said. "We was just playing a little."

"She don't want to play," I said.

"She don't want to?" he said. "She don't want to? She's a fucking whore. Who cares what she don't want to? I paid good money for the little bitch."

"You do what you supposed to?" I said to Billie.

"I done stuff with his pecker and then I fucked him," she said. "He got a ugly little pecker."

"Probably don't see a lot of pretty ones," I said.

The man bent down and took the knife from his boot. It was a big bowie knife with a wide blade. I rapped him on the wrist with both barrels of the shotgun, and the knife clattered to the floor and slid away. The man doubled over, holding his arm against his stomach.

"You cocksucker," he said. "You broke my fucking arm."

I didn't say anything.

"It feels broke," he said.

I didn't say anything.

"You got no right to be banging me with that fucking eight-gauge."

I looked at him and didn't say anything.

"I want my damned money back," he said.

I didn't say anything.

"Ain't you gonna talk?" he said.

"Sure," I said. "First, your arm ain't broke. I can tell. Second, she fucked you, so you don't get your money back. Third, you annoy one whore in this establishment, ever, and I'll kill you."

He stared at me. I stared back. He wanted to say something. But I had, after all, killed Koy Wickman. Still nursing his arm against his stomach, he turned and went to pick up his knife.

"Leave the knife where it is," I said.

He stopped without looking back and stood still.

"I paid eight dollars for that knife," he said finally.

I didn't say anything. He took another step toward the knife on the floor. I cocked the eight-gauge. The sound was bright and clear in the room. He stopped again. I could see his shoulders heave as he took in some air. Then, without looking at me, he turned away from the knife on the floor and walked out of the saloon.

I let the hammers down easy on the shotgun. The pleasant hubbub picked up again. Billie stayed where she was behind my chair.

"What if he comes back," she said.

"He won't," I said.

"What if he gets another knife and comes back. He'll cut me, I know he will."

I looked at her little girl's face with too much make-up on it.

"Got a couch in my room," I said. "You can sleep on it, if you want, till you get to feeling more comfortable."

"I could sleep in the bed," she said. "Be no charge."

I shook my head.

"You're too young for me, Billie," I said.

"I'm twenty years old," she said.

"The hell you are," I said. "You want to stay with me on the couch?"

"Yes."

I fished my room key out of my pants pocket.

"You want to go up now?"

"No," she said. "I want to stay with you."

I nodded.

"Wolfson won't like that so much," I said. "I'm pretty sure he wants his whores working."

"I can't work any more tonight, Everett," Billie said. "I just can't."

I nodded.

"Mr. Wolfson says something, you tell him it's okay," Billie said. "He won't go against you."

"Sure," I said. "Get a chair. If there's any trouble, stay out of my way."

"Yes, Everett," she said. "Thank you."

"You're welcome," I said.

# 7.

Wolfson joined me for breakfast.

"One of my whores is sleeping in your room," he said.

"Yep."

"Meals here are part of the deal," Wolfson said, "but not the girls."

"She's just sleeping there," I said. "I ain't employed her for anything."

"If you ain't fucking her," Wolfson said, "why's she sleeping there?"

"One of her gentleman friends threatened to cut her," I said.

"Didn't you throw him out the other night?"

"Yep."

"You think he'll come back?" Wolfson said.

"Nope, but she does."

"She's scared," Wolfson said.

"Uh-huh."

"And she ain't working," he said.

I shrugged.

"I hired you to help me make money," Wolfson said, "not lose it."

"He cut her up, what would she be worth?"

"Nothing to me," Wolfson said.

"If she run off, what would she be worth?"

Wolfson nodded.

"So you're letting her hide in your room."

"Few days," I said. "Until she ain't scared."

Wolfson nodded.

"Because you're concerned for my best interests," he said.

"Sure."

"And that's why you're looking out for her like this," Wolfson said.

"Nope. I'm looking out for her 'cause I'm softhearted," I said.

Wolfson looked at me maybe. His off eye made it a little hard to say for sure what he was looking at.

"Still ain't carrying her weight," he said.

I nodded.

"Take it outta my pay," I said.

"Christ," Wolfson said. "You are softhearted."

"Uh-huh."

"Didn't seem too softhearted when you blew a hole in Koy Wickman," he said.

"That was business," I said.

"And this ain't," Wolfson said.

"No," I said. "This is softhearted."

"Well, it's business for me," Wolfson said. "I'll take it outta your pay until she's back at work."

I nodded.

"Fuck her if you want," Wolfson said. "You're paying for it anyway."

"Too young for me," I said.

"Says she's twenty," Wolfson said.

"You believe her," I said.

"No."

# 8.

Three days later I had another whore complaint. A customer had tied Short Sally to the bed and left her. One of the other girls had come in to borrow something and found her and cut her loose, and she come running to me.

"Said he wasn't through with me yet," she said. "Told me he was going out with his friends and when they came back, all of them would finish me up."

"He in the room?" I said.

"Finish me up, Everett," Short Sally went on. "That's what he said, finish me up."

"See him in the room?" I said.

Short Sally looked around. She wasn't scared like Billie had been. She was ripping.

"That's him, the fucking pig, there playing faro," she said. "The fat one dressed kinda fancy."

I said, "Come with me, Sal," gave the eight-gauge to one of the bartenders, got down from the chair, and walked over to the faro game.

"This one?" I said.

"Him," she said.

He was wearing a wide-brimmed, low-crowned hat. I took it off his head with my left hand as he started to turn, tossed it on the floor, grabbed a handful of hair with my right hand, and pulled him and the chair over backward.

"Hey," he said.

I let go of his hair and straightened and kicked him in the stomach. He gasped. I stomped on his crotch. He yowled. I reached down and got hold of his collar and started to drag him toward the door. Short Sally ran along beside us, bending over, calling him a "fat cocksucker."

When we got to the door, I dragged him to his feet and pushed him against the doorjamb.

"I see you in here again, I'll kill you," I said.

He shook his head.

Standing beside me, Short Sally spit in his face. I'm not sure he even knew it. I turned him and pushed him through the doorway, put my foot against his butt, and shoved him face-first out into the street. Then I turned and went back to the lookout chair. Short Sally hurried along behind me.

"You shoulda killed him, Everett, the fat bastard, why didn't you kill him like you done Koy Wickman?"

"Can't kill 'em all, Sally."

"Why not? Why can't you?"

The bartender handed me the shotgun and I put it across my lap.

"Never actually quite thought about it, Sally. Killing 'em all just don't seem like a good idea."

"I think it is," she said.

"I can see that, Sal," I said. "But you ain't the one got to do the killing."

# 9.

"What the fuck are you?" Wolfson said. "Fucking Saint Everett of the Whores?"

"Just keepin' order," I said.

"You know who that was you kicked in the balls last night?"

"Can't say that I got his name," I said.

"Name's Greavy," Wolfson said. "Matthew Greavy. He's a county commissioner."

I had a bite of biscuit so I chewed and swallowed before I answered. Wolfson drank some coffee.

"So it's okay if he abuses your whores?" I said when the biscuit was down.

"It's important for me to stay on the right side of the

county," Wolfson said. "I ain't out here looking to sit here in a saloon kitchen for breakfast all my life."

"Pretty good breakfast," I said.

"You know what I mean," Wolfson said. "A business is like a lot of things: It grows or it dies. I plan to grow."

"So maybe you should issue an abuse-my-whores pass to guys like Greavy. Then when I start to kick him in the balls, he can flash the pass, and I stop."

"You being funny?" Wolfson said.

I put some sorghum on another biscuit and ate it.

"I guess not," I said.

Wolfson stood up and walked around the kitchen. The Chinaman was busy chopping onions and paid us no attention. We never talked when he made my breakfast. I didn't understand Chinese. I didn't know if he understood English.

"You're good at your work, Everett," Wolfson said. "Don't know if I ever seen better. You're good with a gun. You're good with your fists. You ain't afraid of much. And people like you. But whores are fucking whores, you understand. They get abused, they get abused. They're used to it."

I nodded.

"You buy what I'm saying?" Wolfson said.

"You're the boss," I said.

"I know that, I want to make sure you know it, too," Wolfson said. "Anytime you think the whores are having problems, you bring them to me."

I nodded and ate some biscuit. I didn't know about his language skills, but the Chinaman made a nice biscuit.

"You buy that?" Wolfson said.

"When I can," I said.

"What do you mean, 'When I can'?"

"Sometimes this kinda work," I said, "you don't have time to consult your employer."

"So you use your own judgment."

"I do," I said.

Wolfson fixed me with his one-and-a-half-eyed stare.

"You do, and it's the wrong judgment, and you'll be out of a job," he said.

"I'd surely miss these biscuits," I said.

# 10.

Maybe Wolfson was right.

It was a Thursday night, raining hard outside, when two wet whores from Polly Patterson's house came into the Blackfoot and sat down at a table near my end of the bar. Wolfson didn't allow any whores but his own in the saloon, so after a minute I took my shotgun, barrels toward the floor, and went and sat down with them.

"Sorry, ladies," I said. "Unaffiliated whores ain't allowed in this establishment."

"You're Everett," one of them said.

I nodded. It was hard to guess age in a whore, but this one looked to be in her forties, and kind of fat. The other girl was younger but no slimmer.

"We heard about you," the older whore said.

I nodded again.

"All good things, I'm sure," I said. "But unaffiliated whores are still not allowed in the Blackfoot."

"We got trouble, Everett," she said. "We need to stay here."

"What kind of trouble?" I said.

Four men in hats and slickers came into the saloon. They stood inside the door, looking around. A couple of them took off their hats and shook the rain off them. Then all four looked at us. I nodded my head at them.

"That kind?" I said.

"Oh, Jesus," the younger whore said.

"The one in front," the older whore said. "With the beard, he paid for one hour with me and Roxanne. We gave him everything he paid for, and when he was through, his friends came in and used us and nobody paid nothing."

"Unaffiliated whores are also not allowed to bring their troubles into this establishment. You steal something to get even?"

Roxanne nodded.

"I got his watch," the older one answered. "And I ain't givin' it back. He owes us more then that."

I nodded. The four men walked over to us.

The guy with the beard said, "These whores with you?"

He didn't look like he washed the beard much.

"They are," I said.

"They don't work here," he said.

"No."

"I thought whores had to work here to be in the saloon."

"I was just discussing that with them," I said. "They been put on notice."

"You throwing them out?" the man said.

He was a thick fella, miner probably, had the sort of over-muscled bow in his back that pick and shovel work can give you.

"I told them I would," I said. "If they ain't out of here by Monday."

"Monday?"

I smiled and nodded.

"Don't tolerate rule-breaking," I said.

The bearded man looked at the shotgun across my lap.

"You Hitch?" he said.

"Yes, sir, I am."

He looked at the shotgun again.

"That an eight-gauge?" he said.

"Yes, sir, it is," I said.

One of the other men said, "Christ. Pellets must look like billiard balls."

"These whores got something belongs to me," the bearded one said.

"You owe us," the older whore said. "You owe us a lot more than we took, don't he, Roxanne?"

Roxanne nodded silently.

"See," the bearded one said. "See, she even admits she took something."

"I don't care," I said.

"She give it back and there won't be no trouble," the bearded one said.

I stood up.

"Or if she don't," I said.

The bearded man didn't seem to know what to say. His three companions shifted uneasily. The whores sat perfectly still.

"You ladies sit right there, where I can see you, make sure you're not stealing any business from our girls," I said. "You gentlemen step to the bar and I'll buy you all a drink 'fore you leave."

The men sort of looked at one another, then at me. Then the bearded man nodded.

"I could use a drink," he said. "Night like this."

# 11.

Place has turned into a fucking sanctuary," Wolfson said.

I shrugged.

"It's not just whores now," he said. "Anybody got trouble comes running into my saloon and waits for you to protect them."

Wolfson was leaning on the bar near my chair, sipping whiskey. He usually drank whiskey through the evening, but it didn't appear to make him drunk. Maybe it was how slow he sipped it.

"For crissake, some guy made a pass at Harley Porter's wife on the street the other day and she hustles right in here to tell you."

"I know," I said. "Maybe if there was a sheriff or some-thing."

"You're turning into the fucking sheriff," Wolfson said.

"Except I ain't," I said.

"No, you ain't," Wolfson said. "You work for me."

"I do," I said.

"Keep that clear in your mind," Wolfson said.

I nodded, watching the room. It was full and lively, the card tables were busy, the bar was crowded. Everything was in good working order. Wolfson sipped his whiskey and looked at the room, too.

"Nice and busy," he said.

He snorted or laughed or something like that. It wasn't a pleasant sound.

"Thing makes me laugh," he said, "is my saloon, a sanc-tuary, like a fucking church or something. People come to my saloon because they feel safe."

"That's not bad for business," I said.

"No," Wolfson said, and made the laugh sound again. "That's what's so funny. I'm busier than I ever been."

At a card table in the middle of the room somebody lost a hand he thought he had won, and got mad and slammed his open hand down on the table. The impact knocked over a bottle of whiskey that rolled off the table and shattered on the floor. The card player whirled toward me and put both hands, palms out, in front of his chest.

"No trouble, Everett. An accident. I'll buy a new bottle."

"That'll be good," I said.

The card player walked to the bar to buy a new bottle. A Chinese man with a broom came from someplace and cleaned up the broken glass.

"Ain't it grand how they love you, Everett," Wolfson said.

"Ever hear of a man named Machiavelli?" I said.

"No."

"When I was at West Point," I said, "they made us read some things he wrote."

"I'm not much for reading," Wolfson said.

"One thing he said sort of stayed with me," I said. "It's better to be feared than loved. Because you can't make them love you. But you can make them fear you."

"Pretty smart fella," Wolfson said. "So what?"

I grinned at him.

"Koy Wickman," I said, "did not die in vain."

# 12.

It was payday at Fort Rucker, and the Blackfoot had a lot more soldiers than usual. They were noisy but peaceful, except for one fight, which I convinced the fighters to take outside. I watched them for a little while as they flailed away drunkenly until one of them threw up and the other walked away in disgust.

I was back in my chair when two men came into the Blackfoot who were not soldiers, or ranch hands, or miners, or lumberjacks, or drummers, or wandering preachers. They had on town clothes and smallish town hats, and they wore guns. In fact, one of them wore two. I always thought two guns were for show. And the fact that his were adorned with bright pearl handles didn't cause me to reconsider. He was as tall as I was, but not as thick, and he wore a big mustache. His partner was shorter and smaller. Kind of scrawny-looking, he was shaved clean, and carried one walnut-handled Colt.

They took a table near the bar and ordered coffee.

We looked at one another.

After a while I said, "You gents new in town?"

The tall one said, "Yes."

We looked at one another some more.

"Passing through?" I said. "Or you planning to stay?"

"We came to do some work for Eamon O'Malley," the tall one said.

"That so," I said. "What kind of work you fellas do?"

The tall one looked at the small one and smiled.

"Hear that, Cato," he said. "Gentleman wants to know what kind of work we do."

The little guy nodded.

"A little of this," he said, "a little of that."

I nodded back, friendly.

"Cato," I said. "Cato Tillson?"

The little guy nodded again. His eyes were sort of narrow, and the upper lids drooped so that the eyes seemed hooded.

"And you'd be Frank Rose?" I said to the tall one.

"You heard of us," he said.

"Cato and Rose," I said.

Rose seemed pleased.

"That's what they call us," he said. "His first name, my last. Kind of funny, huh? How that worked out? Guess people just like the way it sounds."

He sipped some coffee.

"Cato and Rose," he said, enjoying the phrase.

"What's your name?" Cato said.

"Hitch," I said. "Everett Hitch."

"With Virgil Cole awhile, wasn't you?" Cato said.

"I was."

"Never had a chance to go against Cole," Rose said.

"Why you're still here," I said.

Rose laughed.

"I heard he was pretty good," Rose said.

"Best," I said.

"'Course you ain't seen me and Cato work," Rose said.

"Nope."

"Well," Rose said, "maybe you'll get the chance."

"Maybe," I said.

"Either way, we're grateful to you, I guess, for helping us get this job with Eamon."

"By shooting Koy Wickman?"

"Opened up a nice slot for us," Rose said.

"Two of you to replace Koy Wickman?" I said.

Rose grinned some more.

"We're a matched pair," he said. "Both or neither."

He stretched his legs out in front of him and leaned back a little in his chair. The boots were pretty fancy. Like him. He took a cigar from his vest pocket and bit off the tip and lit it, turning it in the flame until it was burning even.

"You know," I said, "I could never figure out why O'Malley needed a gun hand at all, let alone two, let alone two like you."

Rose took a long pull on the cigar and let out the smoke slowly.

"Maybe he figured since Wolfson had you, maybe he should get us," Rose said.

"I'm just a saloon bouncer," I said. "Why's he worried about me?"

"He didn't say."

"Don't make any sense," I said.

"Not much does," Rose said.

I looked at Cato. He appeared to have no view on the matter.

"Ever hear from Cole?" Rose said.

"No."

"Heard he killed a man a little while ago," Rose said.

"Virgil does that sometimes," I said.

"Heard it was over a woman," Rose said.

"In Appaloosa?" I said.

"Yep," Rose said. "Heard he left town right after."

"So he's not marshaling there no more?" I said.

"Don't know," Rose said. "All I heard."

I nodded. Rose and Cato finished their coffee and stood.

"Nice meeting you boys," I said.

"Same here," Rose said.

Cato didn't speak, but he nodded. And the two of them left the saloon. *Allie,* I thought. *Goddamned Allie.*

# 13.

Wolfson and I sat in wicker rockers on the front porch of the hotel next to the saloon and soaked up some early-afternoon sun. At the general store a tired-looking guy with a tired-looking wife and three small kids was loading things onto the back of a buckboard.

"Money in the till," I said, watching the ranch family.

"Sodbusters," Wolfson said. "Probably running a tab, won't be able to pay it, tab gets big enough and I'll own his ranch."

"Why do you want his ranch?" I said.

"Why not," Wolfson said. "Better it should belong to me than him."

"He probably don't feel that way," I said.

"He don't matter," Wolfson said.

I nodded. The three kids were looking at us, staring at my gun. I pretended to draw and shoot at them with my forefinger. They didn't react. Their mother said something and the three of them got up on the back of the buckboard with the groceries. The mother and father got up on the front seat. The father tapped the two mules with the reins, and they moved off south along Main Street.

"You know anything about the two new gun hands Eamon has hired?" Wolfson said.

"Cato and Rose," I said.

"Sounds like a damn circus act," Wolfson said.

"It ain't," I said.

"They good?"

"Very," I said.

"Better than Wickman?"

"Much."

"Better than you?"

"Maybe."

"And there's two of them," Wolfson said.

"Uh-huh."

"They always work together?"

"Far as I know," I said.

"How about Cole?" Wolfson said.

"What about him?"

"How they stack up against him?"

"Never seen nobody stacked up against Virgil Cole," I said.

"Including you?"

"Including me," I said.

"Have you seen Cato and Rose?"

"Not till yesterday," I said.

"So you don't know for sure about them?"

"Never know for sure," I said.

"Maybe we should get Cole up here," Wolfson said.

"You expecting trouble?" I said.

"Why are they here?" Wolfson said.

"Somebody's expecting trouble."

"Or expecting to cause it," Wolfson said.

"What would O'Malley want to cause trouble about?" I said.

"I don't know," Wolfson said.

I didn't quite believe that he didn't know, but I saw no reason to say so.

"Can you get Cole?" Wolfson said.

"Don't know where he is," I said.

"He's not in Appaloosa anymore?"

"That's what I heard."

"How can we find him," Wolfson said.

"Don't think you'll have to," I said. "I expect he might come drifting in here, next few days."

"Here?" Wolfson said. "Why?"

"See me," I said. "Sometimes he likes to talk with me about things."

Wolfson looked like he wanted to ask more, but he didn't quite know what to ask, and I didn't help him out. So he didn't.

Instead, he said, "What are we going to do about Cato and Rose?"

"How about they don't bother us, we don't bother them?" I said.

"They'll bother us," Wolfson said.

"Why do you think so?"

"Eamon wants to be the studhorse around here," Wolfson said.

"And you're in his way?"

"I guess," Wolfson said.

"He runs a mine," I said. "You run this place. How does that put you in his way?"

"Don't know," Wolfson said.

"How about the lumber operation?" I said. "Who's way is that in?"

"Got no idea," Wolfson said.

I didn't believe that, either, but I could see that Wolfson had said all he was going to say on the subject, so I didn't pursue it.

# 14.

I was about to get in my chair in the late afternoon on a Friday, when one of the clerks from the general store came into the saloon.

"Mr. Wolfson wants you in the store," he said. "Bring the shotgun."

The saloon was next to the hotel, and the store was on the other side of the hotel. We walked through the lobby of the hotel to get there. In the store were six men, sodbusters probably, gathered in front of the counter, behind which Wolfson stood with a second clerk. Everybody looked at me when I came in.

One of them said, "And we ain't gonna get scared off by your bully boy, neither."

The speaker was a small, dark, wiry man, with a kind of

sharp angularity about him, like a farming tool. I stopped inside the door and stood against the wall with the shotgun beside my leg, pointing at the floor.

"Make your point, Redmond," Wolfson said.

"You got no right takin' our property," Redmond said.

"I ain't taken your property, Redmond."

"We're all in this together," Redmond said. "You take Pete Simpson's land, it's like takin' mine."

"Simpson owed me money, and he couldn't pay. What am I supposed to do, just give it to him?"

"Give him time. He'll pay," Redmond said. "Thing is, and we all know it here, you don't want him to pay. You want his land. You want all our land."

"I've already made an arrangement for Pete Simpson to stay on his land."

"Sure," Redmond said. "Except now it won't be his land. It'll be your land. And he'll pay you rent."

"Nobody made him run up a bill he couldn't pay," Wolfson said.

I looked at the other sodbusters as Wolfson talked. I wondered which one was Pete Simpson.

"So how's he supposed to feed his cattle, or plant crops, or feed his kids?" Redmond said.

"You know, Bob," Wolfson said, "when you come right on down to it, that ain't my concern. Simpson and I made a business deal and he couldn't hold up his end of it."

"You knew he couldn't when you went into it with him," Redmond said.

He was a fierce little duck, with small, hard eyes on either side of his big plow-blade nose. Wolfson shook his head.

"We're done here, Bob," he said. "This is getting us nowhere."

"We ain't leaving till we get some justice," Redmond said.

Without looking at me, Wolfson said, "Everett."

I nodded and stood away from the wall I'd been leaning on.

"Time to go," I said.

All the sodbusters looked at me. Redmond the hardest.

"You can't shoot us all," Redmond said.

"Actually," I said. "I probably can. Got a big scatter, probably get at least two of you, first shot. Long as I don't get too close."

Nobody said anything. I moved toward Redmond a step.

"I get too close I'll just mangle you."

I stopped.

"'Bout here," I said. "Then I get you and some people near you."

A couple of the other sodbusters began to back up. A fat guy with pink cheeks behind Redmond spoke to him.

"Come on, Bob," he said. "This ain't the way we want it to go. We ain't even got guns."

Somebody else said, "He's right, Bob."

And somebody else said, "Come on, Bob."

And somebody else opened the front door of the store and slowly, one after the other, the sodbusters backed out. Bob Redmond was the last one.

"This ain't over," he said to Wolfson. "This ain't over."

"Nice work, Everett," Wolfson said.

I nodded.

"If they hadn't left would you have shot them?" Wolfson said.

"They left," I said.

"But if they hadn't."

"Sometime maybe they won't leave, then we'll find out," I said.

"It may get rougher," Wolfson said. "I need to know I can count on you."

"So far so good?" I said.

"Yeah," Wolfson said. "I guess so."

I nodded, and grinned at him.

"Bully boy," I said, and walked back to the saloon.

# 15.

Virgil Cole arrived just after sunset on a Monday. He walked into the saloon, a tall man in a dark coat and white shirt wearing a big bone-handled Colt.

He walked to the chair where I was sitting and said, "Evenin', Everett."

"Virgil."

"Thought I might drink some whiskey," he said. "You care to climb down from there and join me?"

"I do," I said.

Virgil ordered a bottle.

"Patrick," I said. "The stuff that Wolfson drinks."

Patrick nodded. Virgil and I sat at a table, and Patrick brought us a bottle and two glasses. Virgil poured.

"Go easy," I said. "Might have to shoot somebody."

"Always a happenstance," Virgil said.

"Heard you left Appaloosa," I said.

"I did," Virgil said.

Wolfson came into the saloon and walked straight to our table.

"Virgil Cole?" he said.

Virgil nodded once.

"I'm Amos Wolfson. I own the place."

Virgil nodded again.

"I've heard a lot about you," Wolfson said. "I'm very proud to meet you."

"How do you do?" Virgil said.

Virgil didn't offer to shake hands. He never shook hands. *No reason to let somebody get hold of you,* he said to me once.

"What brings you to Resolution?" Wolfson said.

"Come to drink a little whiskey with Everett," Virgil said.

Wolfson nodded.

"Bottle's on me," Wolfson said. "And if you're interested in a job, I'd be pleased to offer you one."

Virgil nodded briefly.

"Sure thing," he said. "Right now I'm just going to drink a little whiskey with Everett."

"Sure," Wolfson said, "you bet. Everett, take your time, any trouble one of the bartenders will give a yell."

I nodded.

"Hope to talk with you soon again, Mr. Cole," Wolfson said.

"Thanks for the whiskey," Virgil said.

Wolfson left the table.

"Hard man to look in the eye," Virgil said.

I smiled.

"True," I said.

"Why's he want to hire me?" Virgil said.

"Not exactly sure," I said. "Seems to feel there's trouble coming. Maybe with a fella named Eamon O'Malley, runs a copper mine back a ways in the hills."

"That why he hired you?" Virgil said.

"I don't know, I was looking for work. Maybe he just needed a lookout. Maybe he was planning ahead."

Virgil splashed a little more whiskey in his glass. He held the bottle. I shook my head. He nodded.

"Had any trouble?"

"Had to shoot a local gunny named Wickman," I said. "Worked for O'Malley."

Virgil nodded.

"Anything come of that?" he said.

"Nope."

"Any law here?"

"Not really," I said. "I'm told the sheriff sends a line rider down here every few months. I ain't seen any."

"O'Malley replace the fella you shot?"

"Cato and Rose," I said.

Virgil sat back in his chair a little.

"My, my," he said.

"My thought exactly," I said.

"You talk with them?"

"Yep."

"Anything come of it?"

"Nope."

Virgil appeared to suck on one of his front teeth for a moment.

"Cato and Rose," he said.

"My, my," I said.

We drank a little more whiskey together.

Then Virgil said, "What time's breakfast."

"Kitchen opens up at five-thirty," I said.

"Been a long ride," he said. "I'll turn in."

"See you in the morning," I said.

Virgil nodded and took the bottle and headed out the side entrance of the saloon and into the hotel. I knew he had things to say. But he wasn't ready to say them yet.

# 16.

It was raining in the morning. No wind, and not very cold, with the rain coming straight down and steady. Virgil and I took our coffee outside and sat under the awning on the front porch of the hotel. At the south end of town you could see through the rain how the land sloped down to the plains, where the small ranchers lived. At the north end, where the land rose, the trees were bright green in the wet. The street was muddy and getting worse, and nobody was moving around much. We drank some coffee.

"Small," Virgil said.

"It is," I said.

A single rider hunched in a slicker rode a bay horse toward the livery stable. The rider's collar was up and his hat was pulled down to his ears. The horse's coat was dark and wet with rain. His hooves made a soft sucking sound as he waded through the mud.

"Allie run off," Virgil said.

I nodded. Virgil looked after the horse and rider for a time.

"She run off with fella owned a spread in New Mexico," Virgil said.

I nodded again.

"He didn't have no ranch," Virgil said. "He just tole her that so he could fuck her."

I didn't say anything.

"So he got her as far as Little Springs and dumped her. I found her working in a saloon there."

"Playing piano?" I said.

"No."

I nodded.

"I left her there," Virgil said. "Followed him."

"And?" I said.

"Caught up with him in Three Forks," Virgil said.

"Arrest him?"

"Ain't against the law to fuck Allie," Virgil said.

"No," I said.

The rider turned his horse into the livery stable and out of sight.

"You kill him?" I said.

"Yes," Virgil said.

"He draw on you?"

"Gave him the chance," Virgil said. "He said he wouldn't. Tole him draw or not draw, I was going to shoot him where he stood. He wouldn't draw."

"So you shot him."

"I did," Virgil said.

"How 'bout Allie?"

"I went back to Little Springs, but they tole me she lit out, soon as I went after the tinhorn."

"You go looking for her?" I said.

"No."

"What was the tinhorn's name?" I said, just to be saying something.

"Never did know," Virgil said.

I didn't say anything. I knew what was bothering Virgil. I wondered if he did. Virgil drank the rest of his coffee and went back into the hotel to get some more. I looked at the rain while he was gone. Virgil came out with a full coffee-pot. He poured some in my cup.

"Already got sugar in it," he said.

"Thanks."

"There ranches down there on the plain?" Virgil said.

"Yep."

"Hard to see them through the rain," Virgil said.

"It is," I said.

"I know why you killed Randall Bragg in Appaloosa," Virgil said.

"No reason not to," I said.

"Allie was fucking him, too," Virgil said. "And you knew if I found out I'd have to kill him."

"Something like that."

"You knew he hadn't broken no law," Virgil said.

"Not right then he hadn't."

"But you knew I'd kill him anyway," Virgil said.

"Yes."

"So you done it for me," Virgil said. "So I wouldn't have to."

"I guess."

Virgil took the bone-handled six-shooter out of his holster and looked at it.

"I'm good with this," he said.

"Yes," I said.

"Always been good with it. Made my living most of my life being good with it," Virgil said.

"I know," I said.

"Because most people ain't as good as I am with it," he said.

"So far, none," I said.

He nodded.

"Don't give me the right to go round shooting people," he said. "Just 'cause I can."

"It's good to have a reason," I said.

"I been a lawman," Virgil said. "Never shot nobody 'cept according to the law."

"You always had rules, Virgil."

"Why you shot Bragg for me," Virgil said.

"So you wouldn't have to break your rules," I said. "I didn't mind."

"I appreciate it," Virgil said.

We were quiet. I knew we weren't done with it yet. He was still chewing on it.

"'Cept now I done it," Virgil said. "I shot that tinhorn for fucking Allie."

"And leaving her," I said. "In a whorehouse."

Virgil nodded. "None of that is against the law."

"Might be against some sort of law," I said.

"None I ever seen written down," Virgil said.

"They ain't all written down," I said.

"They are for me," Virgil said.

I had no answer for that. Virgil turned his hand over and looked at the six-gun some more.

"What are you gonna do?" I said after a while.

"I ain't a lawman no more," Virgil said.

"For the moment," I said.

"Nope. Lawman obeys the rules. I broke 'em."

"So what are you gonna do?"

"Hang around here, I guess," he said. "Talk with you."

He moved the gun back and forth in front of him.

"This is all I really know how to do," he said. "Guess I'm a gunman now."

"Wolfson offered you a job," I said.

"Don't know 'bout that yet."

"Either way," I said. "I'll enjoy the company."

"Always helps when I talk with you, Everett," Virgil said.

I grinned at him.

"Virgil," I said. "Ain't you ever noticed that mostly you talk? And mostly I listen?"

He nodded, and looked at me for the first time since we'd sat on the porch.

"Damn," he said. "No wonder I like it so much."

# 17.

Bob Redmond came into the Blackfoot and walked to my end of the bar. He held both hands palms out in front of him as if he were stopping something.

"I don't want no trouble, Hitch," he said.

"Okay."

"I need to talk with you."

"Okay."

"Private," Redmond said.

"You want a drink?" I said.

"I would, in fact," Redmond said.

I gestured to Patrick and he brought a bottle and two glasses. I picked them up and we went to a table. I poured a drink into one glass and pushed it to Redmond. He picked it up and drank it and put the empty glass back down on the table. I poured him another one.

"How 'bout you?" he said.

"Maybe later," I said.

Redmond drank a small amount of his second drink and put it down and leaned forward across the table toward me.

"I got a proposition for you," he said.

I nodded.

"We want to hire you."

"We?" I said.

"The Ranchers Association."

"What do you want to hire me to do?" I said.

"Help us against Wolfson."

"Wouldn't that be sorta awkward?" I said.

"I mean we'd hire you away from him," Redmond said. "We'd pay you more."

"And what would I do to help?" I said.

"Be our gun hand instead of his," Redmond said.

"Until somebody hired me away from you by paying me more," I said.

"No, you couldn't do that."

"If I could do it to him, why couldn't I do it to you?"

"I . . . I don't know what to say."

"Besides," I said. "You hire me away from Wolfson, Wolfson'll hire somebody else."

"But you can stand up to him, whoever he hires. Some of us seen you with Wickman."

"So you hire me away. He hires a replacement. I kill the replacement for you," I said.

"Yes."

"'Less the replacement kills me," I said.

"Goddamn it," Redmond said. "You turn everything I say around."

"Ain't hard to do," I said. "I gather you ain't got many shooters in your association."

"Well, not like you," Redmond said. "I mean, we mostly have a Winchester around, keep the vermin away from the calves, or, I guess, if we had to, to protect ourselves. But we ain't got no professional shooters. Not like you, or them two fellas Eamon O'Malley hired."

"Cato and Rose," I said.

"Yeah. I heard they can take over a town," Redmond said.

"Heard that, too," I said. "Tell me about your problem with Wolfson."

"Well, you heard some of it when you run us out of the store," Redmond said.

"Fella owes him money and don't pay," I said. "What's Wolfson supposed to do."

"That ain't how it is," Redmond said.

"How is it," I said.

Redmond finished his second drink and poured himself another one.

"Most of us grow a few crops for the kitchen, but if we make any money it's from cows. None of us got enough head to matter a hell of a lot, but we sort of pool them, let 'em graze over all our ranges, and then sell them, mostly to Fort

Rucker and the reservation. But we don't deal with the Army, or the Indian agent, there's too many of us, and none of us got enough cattle by ourselves, and the government won't deal with us except through a cattle broker."

"Wolfson?" I said.

Redmond nodded.

"I'm sure he's bribing the Indian agent, maybe the quartermaster at the Fort, too, I don't know. But by the time the deal is done we ain't getting much for our beef. And he's the only broker around. And we got no choice."

"And because you don't have much money, and you got to buy things like flour and coal oil . . ." I said.

"And bridle bits, and horseshoes, and cloth, and nails, and needles, and everything else we can't grow," Redmond said.

"You have to charge it at the Blackfoot Emporium," I finished.

"For way too much, and when we can't pay he takes the land, and we're tenants."

"And there's no other store around," I said.

"Nope."

I smiled.

"The company store," I said.

Redmond nodded. But he didn't smile.

"So what are you trying to do?" I said.

"Just like we can pool our cows, we want to pool ourselves. We ain't big ranchers, but we could be like a big ranch, if we all associated. Then we could broker our own cattle, and maybe establish our own store, and maybe make a living."

"Wolfson probably don't want that to happen," I said.

"'Course he don't," Redmond said. "He's told us that. He says we try organizing like that and we're headed for big trouble."

"Where's O'Malley stand in all this," I said.

"He might help us, he'd do pretty much anything to fuck Wolfson up."

"Why?"

"He wants to replace Wolfson."

"Ah," I said. "That explains Cato and Rose."

"It explains Wickman, too, and it explains you."

"I guess it does," I said. "O'Malley hired Wickman to intimidate Wolfson. So Wolfson hired me to intimidate Wickman. So Eamon doubled down and hired Cato and Rose to intimidate me. Now it's Wolfson's turn."

"If you won't help us," Redmond said, "I guess we got to turn to O'Malley."

"And if O'Malley wins?" I said.

"Maybe it'll be better."

I shook my head.

"Still the same," Redmond said. "Except Eamon be squeezing us 'stead of Wolfson."

I nodded.

"Probably right," Redmond said.

He looked into his nearly empty glass for a time, then finished the drink.

"So will you think about this?" he said.

"I wish you well," I said. "But you need to understand. Fella like me got nothing much that's worth anything, 'cept his gun and his word. When I hired on with Wolfson it's like I sort of gave him my word I wouldn't hire on against him first chance I got."

"I just want the gun," Redmond said.

"Sort of goes with the word," I said.

Redmond nodded.

"I'll talk with O'Malley," he said.

"He'll be no better than Wolfson," I said.

"Can't be worse," Redmond said. "Step at a time."

I nodded.

"You know," Redmond said, "the only safe place in town right now is here?"

I shrugged.

"You seem like you're a decent man, Hitch," Redmond said. "I hope we don't have to go against you."

"We'll see," I said.

# 18.

Virgil and I took the horses out for a ride south of town on a bright morning.

"Ain't good for 'em," Virgil said. "Standing around in the livery all the time, eatin'."

It was low rolling land where the small ranches were, and we let the horses amble.

"Lotta grass," Virgil said.

"Government land mostly," I said. "Ranchers are homesteading."

"They free-range the cattle?" Virgil said.

"They say that they graze them on all the homesteads," I said.

"You believe that?"

"No."

"Never saw government land people didn't free-range," Virgil said.

"Government's a long way away," I said.

"Enough land to support a lot of cattle," Virgil said.

"Homesteaders are trying, I guess, but nobody got the money," I said. "They're talking about organizing."

"Who got the money?" Virgil said.

"Wolfson," I said. "Fella named Eamon O'Malley, runs a copper mine. Probably fella runs the lumber business, Fritz Stark."

"Any of them interested?"

"In a cattle operation?"

"Yeah."

"Don't know," I said. "Ranchers say that Wolfson's trying to run them off their land."

"Tell me 'bout that," Virgil said.

I did.

When I was done Virgil said, "Sounds effectual."

I nodded. We let the horses stop for a time and eat some grass.

"This O'Malley fella," Virgil said. "Think he'll let that happen?"

I shrugged.

"He hired Cato and Rose for something," I said.

"He did," Virgil said.

We pulled the horses back up from the grass and moved on.

"We gonna look for Allie?" I said after a while.

"I guess," Virgil said.

"When?"

"When you get through here," Virgil said.

"I can get through when I want to."

Virgil shook his head.

"Gonna be trouble," he said. "You know it. I know it."

"Might be," I said.

"You ain't going anyplace until that's settled."

"Why not?" I said.

"'Cause you ain't," Virgil said. "Neither would I. It ain't how we are."

"You gonna hang around and wait?" I said.

"Uh-huh."

"'Cause you get lonesome without me?" I said.

"Uh-huh."

"And I listen when you talk," I said.

"Uh-huh."

"And you don't want me to have to go up against Cato and Rose alone."

Virgil grinned at me.

"Uh-huh," he said.

The sun was warm. There was a little breeze. We let the horses drink at a stream that wound down out of the high ground to the north. Then we moved on.

"We go looking for Allie," I said, "where we gonna look?"

"Texas," Virgil said. "She was always talking 'bout Texas."

"Texas is big," I said.

"It is," Virgil said.

"What happens when we find her?"

"We'll see," Virgil said.

"You ain't gonna kill her?"

"No," Virgil said. "Can't kill her. Why I killed him."

I nodded.

"You take up with her again, Virgil," I said, "she'll probably do this again."

"Maybe," Virgil said. "Won't know what's gonna happen next, 'less we find her."

"That would be true," I said.

# 19.

I'm having a drink with Eamon O'Malley this afternoon," Wolfson said to me. "Two o'clock. I'd just as soon you were there."

"Okay," I said.

"Bring the eight-gauge," Wolfson said.

"Sure," I said.

The eight-gauge and I were in the lookout chair by quarter to two. The saloon was nearly empty. Couple of teamsters who had already unloaded and had time to kill until they were reloaded. A rancher whose wife was probably running up a bill at the Blackfoot Emporium. Three lumberjacks who weren't working for whatever reason they had. Wolfson came in through the hotel entrance and went to a table in the front of the saloon two tables from me. He saw me and nodded slightly. There was no one else near us. Patrick brought him a bottle and two glasses.

At two on the hour, Eamon O'Malley came in through the street entrance and walked straight to Wolfson. He didn't have an eight-gauge. But he did have Cato and Rose walking in behind him. Eamon sat down with Wolfson. Cato and Rose leaned on the bar. Rose winked at me. Cato looked at me without expression.

"Amos," Eamon said.

Wolfson nodded.

"Eamon," he said, and gestured toward a chair.

O'Malley sat across from Wolfson.

"Whiskey?" Wolfson said.

"Don't mind if I do," Eamon said.

He picked up the bottle.

"By God," he said, "Bushmills."

"In your honor," Wolfson said.

Eamon poured a full glass.

"Ain't seen whiskey like this since I was in Cheyenne," he said.

"Been saving it," Wolfson said.

He poured a splash for himself.

It was like watching two stallions pretending they didn't want the mares.

Eamon drank some whiskey and smiled.

"Long time," he said, "long time since Ireland."

He looked around the saloon.

"Nice little business you got here, Amos," he said.

"It's a living," Wolfson said.

"Damn good one, if I'm any judge," Eamon said.

"Ain't no copper mine," Wolfson said.

Eamon drank some more whiskey.

"Ahh," he said. "Mining's all overhead until it peters out. This place . . . people keep coming. Town grows, you grow. You got the saloon, the store, the hotel, the bank. Wasn't for me and Fritzie, you'd own the whole place."

"I'd own a lotta headaches," Wolfson said.

Eamon finished his whiskey and poured some more. Wolfson took another very small sip of his.

"Well, you know, that's funny," Eamon said, "funny you should say that. 'Cause I'm here to talk with you about selling to me. You make a nice profit, you don't have any more headaches. You're free to go where you want, do what you want."

Wolfson stared at him.

"You want to buy me out?" he said.

"Yes," Eamon said. "Fair offer."

"Everything?" Wolfson said.

"Saloon, store, hotel, bank, cattle brokerage, everything."

Wolfson stared at him some more.

After a while Eamon said, "Fair offer, Amos."

Still, Wolfson looked at him.

Finally, Wolfson said, "And if I decline the offer?"

Eamon drank some whiskey and glanced over at Cato and Rose.

"Then we'd probably have to insist," Eamon said.

As quiet as I could, I pulled back both hammers on the

eight-gauge. Cato and Rose both heard it. Rose smiled faintly.

"We?" Wolfson said.

Eamon rolled his head to include Cato and Rose.

"Me and some of my friends," he said.

I don't know how. He didn't make any noise. But all of us became aware suddenly that Virgil Cole was standing in the doorway from the hotel. He was motionless, leaning his left shoulder against the doorjamb. Cato Tillson shifted slightly at the bar so as to face Virgil. Rose stayed where he was, looking at me.

"Well, bucko," Eamon said, "who's this?"

It was Cato who answered.

"That's Virgil Cole," Cato said.

The atmosphere in the room had changed. The way it does sometimes before a storm. The uninvolved bystanders in the saloon looked up nervously. Virgil neither moved nor spoke.

Eamon was a little drunk now, which always seemed to me a bad way to do business.

"Well, Virgil Cole be damned," he said. "You want to hear my offer, Amos?"

Wolfson picked up the glass of whiskey and drained it and put the glass down carefully in front of him. He looked at Eamon for a moment without speaking.

Then he said, speaking carefully, "Fuck you, O'Malley."

Eamon's hands were resting on the tabletop. He looked down at them as if they were something new and interesting.

Without looking up, he said, "You don't even want to hear my offer?"

"Fuck you," Wolfson said.

"Onetime offer, Amos," Eamon said.

Wolfson didn't say anything. O'Malley turned and looked over his shoulder at Cato and Rose. He shook his head slightly. Rose looked at me and grinned, and barely shrugged his shoulders. Then O'Malley stood.

"More than one way to skin a cat, Amos," he said.

"Fuck you," Wolfson said.

Eamon nodded thoughtfully for a moment, then he turned and walked out the front door of the saloon, with Cato and Rose behind him.

# 20.

I let the hammers down carefully on the eight-gauge. Wolfson picked up the whiskey bottle and came to the bar. Virgil joined us. Patrick put up three fresh glasses and we drank some of the remaining Bushmills.

"This mean you're willing to work for me?" Wolfson said to Virgil.

Virgil shook his head.

"Nope, just means I'm with Everett."

"Everett works for me," Wolfson said.

"Don't need the money for now," Virgil said. "But I'll stay around, see what develops."

"What do you think?" Wolfson said.

"Hired Cato and Rose for a reason," Virgil said.

"Everett?"

"Agree," I said.

"You'll stick?"

"Yes," I said.

Wolfson looked at Virgil.

"You?" he said.

"I'm with Everett," Virgil said.

"How good are Cato and Rose?" Wolfson said.

"Very," I said.

"Good as you and Cole?" Wolfson said.

"Yet to be determined," Virgil said.

"You think he'll hire some more?" Wolfson said.

"Might," I said.

Wolfson looked at Virgil.

"Might," Virgil said.

"You think I should hire some others?" Wolfson said.

"Going to war, good to have troops," Virgil said.

"Can either of you help me with that?" Wolfson said.

"Probably," I said. "But you got to understand, you hire a bunch of gunmen, you are not hiring from the top of the pile."

"They be trouble?" Wolfson said.

"Sure," Virgil said.

"Will I be able to count on them?" Wolfson said.

"No," Virgil said.

"Most shooters ain't too disciplined," I said. "Where's Stark stand in all this?"

"I think Fritzie just wants to cut lumber and sell it," Wolfson said.

"And the ranchers?" I said.

"They don't count for much," Wolfson said.

"They might if they got together and took a side," I said.

"Hell," Wolfson said, "so would the chickens if they ganged up on the rooster."

"Well," I said. "First thing, I guess, would be to see if Eamon's hiring."

"And if he is?" Wolfson said.

"Maybe you start hiring, too. Virgil and I can sort of sift through them."

"And if you don't like them?"

"We'll fire them," I said.

"Where do I start?" Wolfson said.

I looked at Virgil.

"I was you," Virgil said, "I'd see a fella named Willy Beck in Araby."

"I say you sent me?" Wolfson said.

Virgil smiled a little.

"Sure," he said.

Wolfson stepped away from the bar.

"You sure this ain't just some kind of a business offer and that'll be the end of it?"

"'More than one way to skin a cat, Amos,'" I said.

He nodded.

"Bottle's yours," he said, and walked away.

We each added a little to our glasses.

"Elegant whiskey," Virgil said.

"Why not take his money?" I said. "You'll maybe end up fighting his battle?"

"Don't want it," Virgil said.

"Why not?" I said.

"More comfortable if I'm helping my friend," Virgil said.

I sipped my whiskey.

"'Cause you ain't a lawman anymore," I said.

"Ain't clear to me right now what I am," Virgil said.

"You're good with firearms," I said.

Virgil nodded and drank some whiskey.

"And you're my friend," I said.

Virgil nodded again.

"We'll see about the rest," he said.

# 21.

It had been hot all week, so that when the rain came on Thursday night everyone was pleased. Zorn Tully came in, shook the rain off of his round hat, and offered to buy drinks for everyone. No one declined.

"What's the celebration?" Patrick said when he finished putting the drinks out and Zorn had paid him.

"Leaving town," Zorn said. "Just wanted to say good-bye to everyone before I went."

"Where you going?" Patrick said.

"Maybe Laramie," Zorn said. "Maybe Denver. Ain't sure yet. Never been to Denver."

"How come you're going?" Patrick said.

"Sold my saloon," Zorn said.

"You sold the Excelsior?"

"Yep, Eamon O'Malley bought it."

"O'Malley?" Patrick said.

"Yep."

"He give you a good price?" Patrick said.

"Fair," Zorn said. "It was a fair price."

The Excelsior Saloon was directly across the street from the Blackfoot.

"How come you decided to sell," I said.

"Been here long enough," Zorn said. "Fella came along, offered me a good fair price, I took it."

"Much negotiating?" I said.

"No, like I say. Eamon came in, offered a good fair price."

"Anyone come with him?" I said.

Zorn didn't look at them.

"Sure," he said. "Couple fellas work for him."

I nodded.

"Cato and Rose?" I said.

Zorn sort of shrugged.

"Yeah," he said. "I believe so."

"Good negotiators," I said.

"Good fair price," Zorn said.

He was not just avoiding my eyes now. He was looking at something across the room. I looked, too. Just inside the saloon door, Cato and Rose stood looking at us.

Zorn began to move away from the bar.

"Everett," Zorn said, "been good knowing you. I tole Patrick to give you one on me when you get off."

I nodded, and Zorn Tully walked rapidly away from the bar and out the side door of the saloon where it connects with the hotel. I watched him go. Then I looked over at Cato and Rose. Rose grinned at me and shrugged and walked over. Cato stayed by the door.

"Heard Tully was buying drinks," Rose said. "Guess we got here too late."

"Said he was leaving town," I said.

"I believe he is," Rose said. "He tell you he sold his saloon?"

"He mentioned it," I said.

"He tell you he sold it to Eamon O'Malley?"

"He mentioned that, too," I said.

"Right across the street," Rose said. "Kinda funny, ain't it?"

"What's funny?" I said.

"This little dump of a nowhere town," Rose said. "On this side of the street, the saloon bouncers are you and Virgil Cole. On the other side of the street, the saloon bouncers gonna be me and Cato."

"You're right," I said. "Lotta talent, for a little town."

"More coming," Rose said.

# 22.

"Fair offer, my ass," Wolfson said. "That cheap Irish fuck has never made anyone a fair offer in his life. You saw the way he tried to buy this place."

It was late. The saloon was closed. Virgil and I sat with Wolfson at a table and had a drink.

"You think he paid him anything?" I said.

"Cash," Virgil said. "Show money. Not much, but all cash, so it felt like something."

Wolfson nodded slowly.

"Like a reservation buck," he said. "On a binge."

He poured himself another drink, offered the bottle toward Virgil and me. We both shook our heads.

"It's starting," Wolfson said.

"You and O'Malley?" I said.

"Yes."

"Might be," I said.

"You'll stay," he said.

"Yes," I said.

Virgil said, "I'm with Hitch."

"Think it's time I should see that fella in Araby?"

"Willy Beck?" Virgil said.

"Why not?" I said.

"You agree with me?" Wolfson said. "This is not going to stop?"

"Not right away," Virgil said.

"Frank Rose hinted to me that they were hiring."

"God," Wolfson said. "It's like a damned war starting."

Virgil and I were quiet.

"Why is he so crazy to take over?" Wolfson said. "A fucking war, for crissake!"

"Remember what he said, when he made the offer? A mine is all overhead until it peters out."

"He wants overhead," Wolfson said. "I'll show him fucking overhead. He's making big, big money up there."

"Until it peters out," I said.

Wolfson stared at me.

"You think it's petering out?"

"He seems eager to get into a new business," I said.

"Goddamn," Wolfson said. "Goddamn."

He poured more whiskey. Virgil and I declined again.

"He's petering out, and we can hold him off long enough he'll run out of money," Wolfson said. "Will Cato and Rose stick with him if there's no money?"

"No," Virgil said.

"Nobody else he hires, either," I said.

"So we hold him off he'll have to quit."

"He knows that, too," Virgil said.

"Meaning?" Wolfson said.

"Meaning he'll push pretty hard to get it done 'fore that happens," I said.

# 23.

Me and Virgil were sitting on the front porch of the Blackfoot Hotel. Across the street at Zorn Tully's old saloon, there was a new sign in place that read *O'Malley's New Excelsior*. There was a lot of traffic on the street. Horsemen coming in, mostly. Some of them Eamon's. Some of them ours.

"You ever heard about the Battle of Waterloo?" I said to Virgil.

"In Europe?" Virgil said.

"Uh-huh. The Duke of Wellington defeated Napoléon there."

"Napoléon was the Empire of France, wasn't he?"

"Something like that," I said.

I knew he meant emperor.

"When I was at the Academy," I said, "we had to read about it. The Duke's army was full of riffraff, a lot of them had been grabbed off the street by press gangs, a lot of them been let out of prison to fight."

Virgil nodded, watching the horsemen.

"So," I said. "Somebody asks the Duke before the battle how he feels about his army. And he says, 'I don't know if they will scare the French, but they scare the hell out of me.'"

Virgil smiled and nodded as he watched the horsemen. Three riders pulled up in front of where we were sitting. The one closest to us was a kid with his hat brim turned up in front, and a feeble-looking little beard starting on his face. He had a Winchester in the saddle boot, and a big showy Colt with a white handle on his hip.

"You Virgil Cole?" he said.

"I am," Virgil said.

"I heard you was the best," the kid said.

Virgil shrugged.

"So far," he said.

"My name's Henry Boyle," the kid said.

Virgil nodded.

"Lotta people claim I'm as good as anybody," the kid said.

"Nice to know," Virgil said.

"You working for Wolfson?" the kid said.

"I'm with Hitch," Virgil said.

"Hitch working for Wolfson?"

"I am," I said.

"Well, we're on the same side, I guess," the kid said.

Virgil said nothing.

The kid looked at Virgil. Virgil looked back. The kid glanced at the other two riders. They didn't have anything to say. The kid looked back at Virgil, then at me. Nobody had anything to say.

"Well, nice talking to you," the kid said.

Virgil nodded. The three riders moved on toward the livery.

"What the fuck is Willy Beck sending us?" I said.

"Not much," Virgil said.

"I'll bet Wolfson haggled on price," I said.

Virgil looked after the departing Henry Boyle.

"And lost," Virgil said.

# 24.

Bob Redmond walked up the board sidewalk toward the front porch of the Blackfoot.

"Mind if I sit?" he said.

Virgil didn't respond, and I realized that I had assumed he would. It was funny, me and Virgil these days. Always before, he'd been in charge. Always before, I had worked for him. Now I wasn't sure if I was in charge, and he didn't exactly work for me. But things were different.

"Don't mind," I said. "This is Virgil Cole."

"I heard of you," Redmond said.

Virgil nodded.

"You working for Wolfson now?" Redmond said.

"Visiting Everett," Virgil said.

"But if there was trouble?"

"You think there'll be trouble?" Virgil said.

"It's coming," Redmond said. "Sure as hell."

"Wolfson and O'Malley?" I said.

"O'Malley came and talked with us last night," Redmond said.

"Who's us?" I said.

"Ranchers, said there was trouble coming. Said we're either with him or with Wolfson. Tole us if he ran things we'd get a fair shake on the beef prices, and a decent rate at the bank."

"He want your help?" I said.

"I don't know," Redmond said. "My sense is that he just don't want us, you know, sniping at his flank."

"How many ranchers," Virgil said.

"All told maybe fifty."

"How many at the meetin'?" Virgil said.

Redmond paused and counted in his head.

"Me and six others," he said.

Virgil didn't say anything.

"We're scattered," Redmond said. "We work hard. Lot of us can't get to meetin's."

"You speak for them all?" I said.

"I don't know. Yeah, I guess I do. Nobody else does."

"What do you want out of this?" I said.

"We got to get rid of Wolfson," Redmond said. "He's chokin' us. We can't make it with Wolfson running things."

"And you think you can with O'Malley?" I said.

"No."

"So?"

Redmond was quiet for a minute.

"We got to get rid of Wolfson," he said.

"So you're throwin' in with him," I said.

"I guess so, 'less you could help us."

"How we gonna do that?" I said.

Redmond was sitting with his feet flat on the floor, his elbows resting on his thighs, his hands clasped. He stared down at the clasped hands for a time.

"What would work for us," he said, "would be the two of them fight it out, and after they beat hell out of each other, and one of them finally wins, we take the town away from him."

Redmond looked up at us. Virgil smiled.

"Nice," Virgil said.

"Might need more than a few Winchesters for that," I said.

"I know."

"Got the balls for it?" Virgil said.

Again, Redmond looked at his hands for a while.

"No, I don't think we do," he said.

"Only a fool would have claimed they did," I said. "It's sort of special work."

"But if you could help us, especially with Mr. Cole here. We couldn't pay you much now, but . . ."

I put up my hand.

"Same answer as before. I work for Wolfson."

"Mr. Cole doesn't," Redmond said.

"I'm with Everett," Virgil said.

We all sat silently.

Finally, Redmond said, "Well, we can't live the way we're living."

"You can count on changing that," Virgil said.

# 25.

Virgil and I rode out in the morning to visit Fritz Stark at his sawmill. We had some strong coffee with him in the raw-plank shack that served as an office at the mill. The sound of the steam saw and the smell of sawn wood permeated everything.

"Name's Everett Hitch," I said. "He's Virgil Cole."

Stark was a tall, sharp-edged man with thick eyebrows and no social grace.

"What do you want?" he said.

"Wanted to talk," I said.

"Go ahead," Stark said.

"You probably know there's trouble brewing in town," I said.

"Never go to town," Stark said. "Don't know nothing 'bout it."

"You know Wolfson?" I said. "Runs the emporium? O'Malley, who owns the copper mine?"

"Know 'em," Stark said. "Don't like 'em."

"Why not?" I said.

"Coupla thievin' cocksuckers," Stark said.

"How about a young fella named Redmond?" I said.

"Don't know him," Stark said.

"If Wolfson and O'Malley got into some sort of shooting situation, would you back one against the other."

"No," Stark said.

He looked at Virgil.

"What's your name again?" Stark said.

Virgil smiled. I could tell he liked Stark.

"Cole," he said. "Virgil Cole."

Stark nodded to himself.

"What I thought," Stark said. "I know about you."

"Uh-huh," Virgil said.

"You're a lawman," Stark said.

"Used to be," Virgil said.

"What are you now?" Stark said.

"Don't know," Virgil said.

"You up here working for somebody?" Stark said.

"Nope," Virgil said.

"So why you here?" Stark said.

"Visiting Everett," Virgil said.

"How 'bout you," Stark said. "You a lawman?"

"Used to be," I said.

"What are you now," Stark said.

"I keep the peace in Wolfson's saloon," I said.

"Wolfson send you up here?"

"Nope."

"So why you up here talking to me?" Stark said.

"Curious by nature," I said.

"Well, I ain't," Stark said. "I just want to cut my lumber and stack it on the flatbed."

"And you don't plan to take sides," I said, "if there's trouble between 'em."

"Hope they kill each other," Stark said. "Got no use for either one."

I stood.

"Thanks for your time," I said.

"Well, I ain't got much of it," Stark said. "You want somethin' to eat 'fore you go?"

I said, "No thanks."

Virgil grinned.

"Your coffee's so chewy," he said. "It's a full meal by itself."

# 26.

We rode slowly down out of the trees toward Resolution, letting the horses pretty well take us.

"Might be easier world," Virgil said, "everybody was like Stark."

"Might not be much fun," I said.

"True," Virgil said. "But he knows what he is. He's a fella cuts lumber."

"Yep."

"I been reading a lot," Virgil said.

"You do that," I said.

"Like to try and learn stuff," Virgil said. "I'm reading this fella Locke. You know, the English fella."

"They told us about him at the Academy," I said.

"You sure don't talk like a fella went to West Point," Virgil said.

"Been riding with you too long," I said.

"Been good for you," Virgil said.

"Maybe," I said.

"This Locke," Virgil said. "If I'm readin' him right, he says that the law is sort of a contract between the people and the government."

"Uh-huh."

"So if either side breaks the contract," Virgil said, "what happens?"

"I don't know."

The horses paused hock-deep in a small stream and drank some water.

"What I was wondering," Virgil said, "when we was marshaling in Appaloosa, was we the government or the people."

"Virgil," I said, "mostly what I remember from the Academy is cavalry tactics."

The horses stopped drinking and moved on.

"Well, I been thinking about that," Virgil said.

"I know," I said.

"I broke the contract," Virgil said.

"You think so?" I said.

"Ain't that what happened?" Virgil said. "I hired on to be the law, and I wasn't."

"Mostly you were," I said.

"Mostly is okay for sodbusters," Virgil said, "or miners, but when you're a gunman . . ."

The horses plodded out of the tree cover and onto the cleared slope above the town.

"Wouldn'ta been no law," I said, "in Appaloosa, wasn't for you."

Virgil didn't answer.

Heading toward the town and the livery and maybe some feed, the horses started to move a little faster.

"Virgil," I said, "ever since I know you, you been dividing everything into legal and illegal. Maybe there's other ways to think about it. Everybody don't go around thinking like that."

We rode in silence for a little.

Then Virgil said, "I ain't everybody, Everett. I kill people."

# 27.

There was an old wooden barrel set on its end out there. Beside it was a pile of empty tin cans. There were five cans on top of the barrel. Arrayed about twenty-five yards away from the barrel were the troops of Wolfson's new army. It was a sorrowful-looking group. But I'd seen some of O'Malley's, and they were no better. We had a guy fired from the Pinkertons, a former shotgun messenger, two buffalo skinners who still smelled of it, a guy who'd been a deputy sheriff in Lincoln County, couple of guys who'd been in the Army, some others whose history I never did know, and out front and noisy, Henry Boyle.

"We need to see you shoot," I said to the troops.

"You needs to see me shoot?" Boyle said. "You don't know about me already?"

"Need to see it," I said.

"I ain't wasting my time on tin cans," he said.

He looked around at his fellow soldiers and grinned widely.

"Whyn't you fellas just trot me out a sodbuster or two?" he said.

He went into a sudden crouch and drew and pretended to shoot at a sodbuster. The draw was very quick. He slid the Colt back in its holster and straightened up, still playing to the other troops.

"Okay?"

I looked at Virgil. He nodded and walked in front of the army with his back to the barrel twenty-five yards away. He turned easily, drew his gun comfortably, and shot all five cans off the barrel. He opened the cylinder, took out the spent rounds, put in five fresh ones, and closed the cylinder. Everybody stared at him.

"Can you do that?" Virgil said to Boyle.

One of the odd things about seeing Virgil Cole shoot was that he never looked fast; everything looked sort of comfortable and relaxed. But I who had seen him shoot for real many times knew that however slow he looked, he was always just a little faster than the man he was shooting against. Since I had known him, no one had ever beaten him. A kid like Boyle would know the reputation, but he'd be puzzled by the fact that Virgil didn't seem quick.

"That wasn't fast," Boyle said.

Virgil walked down to the barrel and put five new cans up.

"Accurate's good," Virgil said. "Whyn't you shoot?"

The kid made a sort of scornful laugh and went into his crouch, did his fast draw, and knocked down two of the five cans.

"That was fast," the kid said.

"Sure," Virgil said, "and you missed three out of five. They was men shooting back, you'd be dead."

"And you'da been dead 'fore you got the damn firearm out of the holster, for crissake," Boyle said. "I could hit them all like you did, if I was as slow as you was."

Virgil nodded and walked to the barrel. He set two new cans up beside the three that Boyle had missed. Then he walked back and stood beside Boyle.

"We'll shoot together," Virgil said. "I say I can knock all five cans down, 'fore you can get off a shot."

"You're crazy," Boyle said.

"Everett?" Virgil said. "You wanna call it."

I nodded.

"When I say 'go,' you shoot."

Boyle went into his crouch, his hand curled, waiting near the gun butt. Virgil stood motionless, like he was waiting for a train. The troops were quiet. The wind was still. Somewhere I could hear the sound of a locust.

I said, "Go."

With a leisurely movement, Virgil shot all five cans while Boyle was drawing. He opened the cylinder, took out the spent shells, put in the new ones, closed the cylinder, and slid the gun back into his holster. No one made a sound. It seemed as if in the intensity of the silence you could still hear the gunshots. Boyle stood holding his gun half-raised.

Boyle said, "You . . . you can't do that again."

"Sure I can," Virgil said.

"You . . ."

"First thing you boys want to do," I said to the troops, "is hit the target. Second thing is to do it quick. But quick don't matter if you don't hit what you're quick at."

"Can you do that?" Boyle said to me.

"Pretty close," I said.

"But not as pretty," Virgil said. "Think about it. Everett and me been doing this shooting thing for quite some time. And we're both still here. Must mean something."

"I . . . goddamn, I never seen anything like that."

"Lotta things you maybe never seen," Virgil said. "Don't mean they can't happen. You was shooting against me for real, you'd have five bullets in your chest now."

"Fuck," Boyle said. "It was only a bunch of cans. The real thing is different."

"Sure," Virgil said.

Boyle holstered his piece and walked away.

"Okay," I said. "Let's shoot. Take your time. Handgun, rifle, whatever you're comfortable with."

The new troops began firing. The ex-soldiers used Winchesters and had an easier time of it. The former deputy was pretty good with a Colt. And the Pinkerton guy. The shotgun messenger used a shotgun and had the easiest time of all. The two skinners couldn't hit the barrel with handguns, let alone the cans.

"We'll get you boys shotguns," Virgil said.

When it was over, the former deputy from Lincoln County walked over to Virgil.

"That's the best shooting I ever seen," he said.

Virgil nodded and smiled at him.

"Yeah," he said. "I know."

# 28.

Wolfson's army was sleeping in his hotel, eating in his dining room, and drinking in his saloon. Except for Cato and Rose, who stayed in town upstairs at the Excelsior, O'Malley's forces were domiciled at the mine. They didn't have anything to do until the fight started, so they spent a lot of time in the New Excelsior. From across the street, O'Malley's army didn't look like much of an improvement on ours.

"Be a kindness to the world," Virgil said, "to let them fight to the death."

"Wouldn't be a loss," I said.

We were sitting on the front porch of the hotel, with our feet up on the rail.

"So," Virgil said. "Wolfson's got his army and O'Malley's got his army. What happens now?"

"I don't think they know," I said. "Either one of them."

"And the sodbusters?" Virgil said.

"They say they're backing O'Malley."

"That mean," Virgil said, "they're buckling up, riding on in?"

"Don't know," I said. "Don't think they know."

"They can't keep paying these people to sit around and get drunk," Virgil said. "Somebody going to have to do something."

"I know."

"Sodbusters were smart, they'd stay out of it until they see who wins," Virgil said.

"They ain't smart," I said.

"Neither is anybody else," Virgil said.

The Chinese cook came out of the hotel carrying biscuits and coffee on a tray. He put the tray down on the floor between us and went back in. I poured us some coffee.

"Chink ever say anything?" Virgil said.

"No," I said.

"Does what he does, and keep his mouth shut," Virgil said.

"He does," I said.

"He's smart," Virgil said.

Across the street, Cato and Rose came out of the New Excelsior and sat down on its porch. Rose pretended to shoot us with his forefinger. Cato simply looked at us. I nodded at them.

"Why do you suppose they're in town?" I said.

"Keep their troops from trashing the saloon," Virgil said.

I nodded.

"It's a problem," I said.

Henry Boyle came walking up the street from the livery stable and turned into the saloon. He didn't look at us as he passed.

"Speaking of problems," I said.

"I embarrassed him at the can shoot."

"You were trying to warn him," I said.

Virgil shrugged.

"Now he gotta prove something," Virgil said. "To me, to himself, to his friends. Maybe all of that."

"Could be we'll have to kill him," I said.

"Probably will," Virgil said.

We drank coffee. The cook had sweetened it already.

"Maybe we should fold it up here, Virgil," I said. "And go to Texas."

He shook his head.

"Why?" I said. "What do you care. You're just helping me out."

Virgil shook his head again. I looked at him for a moment.

"You want to see it through," I said.

"Might as well," he said.

I looked at him some more.

"You're figuring yourself out," I said.

Virgil shrugged.

"Instead of enforcing the law," I said, "you're helping out your friend."

"Might be," he said.

"Rules of friendship instead of the rules of law."

"I guess," Virgil said.

"You slick sonovabitch," I said. "You're using this fight to see what you are when you're not a lawman."

"Useful to know," Virgil said.

"And after that," I said, "we'll go to Texas."

"Sure," Virgil said.

He looked at me for a long moment. Then he said, "Friendship's real."

"Yeah," I said. "I know."

"Wouldn't work if it wasn't," Virgil said.

I nodded.

"Know that, too," I said.

# 29.

Between engagements, Billie liked to stand by the street door and keep an eye out for clients. It was early in the evening, still light outside, and Billie at the door, when there were a couple of shots fired in the street.

"Everett," Billie shouted. "There's trouble outside."

"Not my problem," I said.

"No, but you might want to watch," she said. "Fancy Guns Boyle just put a couple bullets through the front window at the Excelsior."

"My goodness," I said, and got down from my chair and walked over and stood.

In the street was Henry Boyle, obviously drunk, with four more of our army, also obviously drunk. He was waving his gun at the saloon.

"Fuck the Excelsior," Boyle hollered. "Fuck O'Malley and the Excelsior."

He had some trouble saying "Excelsior." While he was struggling with it, Frank Rose came out of the Excelsior, and Cato Tillson behind him. Rose moved right a few steps, Cato left.

"You doing the shooting?" Rose said.

"You bet your ass," Boyle said. "Me, Henry Hackworth Boyle."

Rose looked amused, and without taking his eyes off Boyle, he said to Cato, "Hackworth."

Cato nodded.

Virgil Cole had come up to stand with us. Virgil rarely made any noise when he walked.

"Well, well," he said.

"Maybe we won't have to kill him after all," I said.

"How come you shooting holes in our window," Rose said.

His voice was amused, as if he was having some fun with a mischievous boy.

"'Cause O'Malley owns it, and I'm with Wolfson."

Rose nodded.

"He's with Wolfson," Rose said to Cato.

Cato didn't speak.

"Lucky Wolfson," Rose said, and smiled.

Boyle misunderstood Rose's pleasantness. The mild tone made him feel even braver.

"So you fellas gonna do something about it?" he said.

Rose grinned.

"Yes," he said. "As a matter of fact, Hackworth, we are."

The drunks around Boyle began to move away from him. Boyle looked like he was trying to focus.

"What are you gonna do?" he said.

"We're probably gonna shoot you, Hackworth," Rose said.

"I got my gun right out," Boyle said, and waved it at them. "What if I shoot you first?"

"Don't make much difference, Hackworth," Rose said. "Don't figure, drunk as you are, you can hit either one of us, assuming you got the balls to actually try."

"I got the balls," Boyle said. "I got the balls. Don't you think I don't."

Rose nodded indulgently.

"Maybe you do. And maybe you even hit one of us," Rose said, smiling faintly, "the other one kills you."

Boyle's support moved farther away from him. Boyle frowned as if he was trying to concentrate. Rose stepped down off the porch of the Excelsior and began to walk toward Boyle.

"It occurs to me, Cato," Rose said as he walked toward Boyle, "whoever shoots Hackworth got to go in later and clean the weapon."

Cato nodded.

Boyle began slowly to back away as Rose walked toward him. He seemed not to know that he was doing it.

"I hate to clean a weapon," Rose said. "Don't you, Cato?"

Cato nodded again.

Rose reached Boyle, and suddenly his gun was in his hand

and he brought it down hard across Boyle's forearm. Boyle yelped, and his gun spun into the street. The fading remnants of Boyle's supporters departed.

Rose's gun was back in its holster. Boyle was hunched over, nursing his forearm against him. Rose took hold of Boyle's shoulders, turned him, and kicked him in the backside.

"Go home, Hackworth," he said.

"If I was sober," Boyle muttered.

"You was sober," Rose said, "you'd be dead. Me and Cato don't take much pleasure shooting drunks, 'less we have to."

Boyle looked at his gun lying in the street.

"Leave it," Rose said.

"What am I supposed to do without a gun?" Boyle said. His voice was petulant.

"Far as I can see," Rose said, "whether you got a gun or not don't make much difference."

Still holding his bruised arm, Boyle looked for a moment longer at the gun. Rose took hold of his shirt collar in the back and shoved him toward the hotel. Boyle stumbled a couple of steps and slowed and got himself organized, and walked clumsily across the street toward the Blackfoot Hotel.

Rose looked over at the Blackfoot Saloon and saw us and smiled and made a thumbs-up gesture. I nodded. Then he went back up onto the porch, and he and Cato went back into the Excelsior.

"Too bad," Virgil said to me. "Somebody's gonna have to kill him. Woulda been convenient if it was them."

# 30.

Her last client had left, and Billie's evening was over. She sat with me and Virgil in the back of the Blackfoot and drank some whiskey thinned with water.

"How come that fool did that," Billie said.

"Henry Boyle?" I said.

"Yes. How come he tried to go up against Cato and Rose."

"Drunk," I said.

Virgil shook his head.

"Scared," he said.

"Scared and drunk," I said.

Virgil nodded.

"Probably a connection," he said.

"But if he was sacred," Billie said, "why did he start trouble?"

"Seen a lot of kids like that," Virgil said. "Killed some. They grow up scared and they think if they had a gun maybe they wouldn't be scared. So they get a gun and they half learn to use it, and maybe they shoot a couple of drunks more scared than they are, and they think they are gunmen. They ain't. What they are is still scared."

"If I could shoot like you," Billie said, "either one of you, I would never be scared of nothin'."

Virgil grinned.

"I wasn't scared 'fore I ever had a gun," he said.

It startled me. Not the business about being scared and not scared. I understood that. It was just that I couldn't imagine Virgil without a gun. As long as I'd known him, Virgil had been exactly what he was. Which was Virgil Cole. I couldn't imagine him as anything else.

"I bet I'd feel a lot safer with a gun," Billie said.

"And you'd have reason to," Virgil said. "But you ain't brave without a gun, you ain't brave."

"But Henry Boyle don't know that," I said to Billie. "You make a living doing gun work, you got to accept the possibility somebody gonna shoot you dead."

"No matter how good you are?" Billie said.

"No matter how good," I said.

Billie nodded.

"So you have to be brave anyway," she said.

Virgil and I both nodded.

"Or at least calm," Virgil said. "Calm's probably better than quick, and scared don't make you calm."

"Henry can shoot a lot better than most," I said. "'Cause

most can't shoot at all. But it's not enough for him. Unless he can be the best, he has no peace of mind."

"And he's not the best," Billie said.

"Nowhere near," I said. "And if he ain't the best, then he ain't safe. Somebody might kill him."

"He got embarrassed at target practice the other day. So he got drunk and went off on Frank Rose and Cato Tillson. It coulda got him killed. But instead it got him humiliated again. Now he'll have to do something else, 'cause he can't stand feeling the way he does."

"Why?" Billie said.

"Don't know," Virgil said.

"Most of the people start trouble like that are scared," I said. "Wickman was scared."

"It's funny, you know? If you boys are right, then the way you know a guy's not scared is if he don't start trouble. And the way you know he is is if he does."

"Some truth to it," Virgil said. "You know what you can do, and you know that you're willing to do it, and you don't have to show anybody anything. It's kind of calming."

"I don't know, though," Billie said. "I'm scared. I get humiliated. I don't start a lot of trouble."

"Maybe you ain't as scared as you think," Virgil said.

"And you ain't a man," I said.

"I wasn't sure you knew that," Billie said.

"Being a man in these parts can pressure you some," Virgil said.

# 31.

Virgil sat alone near the back of the saloon sipping a
beer, looking at nothing, and seeing everything, the
way he did. Wolfson was eating supper at the bar. He seemed
in a hurry to finish. After he finished his supper, Wolfson
strolled over to me in the lookout chair.

"Want you to be sure and stay close tonight," he said.
"Cole, too."

"Can't speak for Virgil, but I'll be here."

"Which means he'll be here, too," Wolfson said. "Maybe
you could speak to him when we're through talking here."

I nodded and said, "You expecting trouble?"

Wolfson smiled and leaned closer to me.

"Sent some boys out to O'Malley's to hit him tonight,"
Wolfson said, "when he ain't ready for it."

"And Cato and Rose are at the Excelsior," I said.

"Yep."

"And you kept me and Virgil here?" I said.

"Case it doesn't work, I'll need protection."

"What are the boys planning on doing when they get there?" I said.

"Killin' every last soul," Wolfson said.

"Who's leadin' 'em?"

"Boyle," Wolfson said.

I didn't say anything.

"He's perfect for the job," Wolfson said. "Couldn't wait."

"Bet he couldn't," I said.

"I mean, ain't every man ready to go out and kill twenty people for no reason 'cept I told him," Wolfson said.

"Probably a good thing," I said.

"Oh . . . yeah," Wolfson said. "Sure. Boyle's a fucking lizard. But when you're at war with a bunch of fucking lizards, fella like him is handy."

"You know Cato Tillson backed him down on the street the other night," I said.

"Heard about that," Wolfson said. "Boyle claims he was too drunk to see, let alone fight."

I nodded.

"Probably so," I said.

"Okay, stay close," Wolfson said. "Might have some high celebrating later on."

"What about the miners?" I said.

"A few could get hurt, I suppose," Wolfson said. "Can't be helped if they do. We're in a fucking war, you know."

"Right," I said.

"I'll be here in the saloon, until the boys come back," Wolfson said. "Speak to Cole. I want you and him watching me tight."

"Sure," I said.

Wolfson gestured to Patrick, who handed him a bottle and a glass. Wolfson took it and sat near the bar at a table where I could see him.

Wasn't a bad plan, if you don't mind back-shooting twenty men, who would probably have back-shot you first if they'd thought of it before you did. If it worked, it would end Wolfson's troubles right then, and leave him in charge of the town with twenty gun hands to back him.

I climbed down from the chair, took the eight-gauge with me, and went to talk with Virgil.

# 32.

Henry Boyle came into the Blackfoot about an hour later. His eyes were big and his face was flushed. He held the saloon doors open and behind him came the two buffalo skinners carrying a body, which they dropped on the floor near the bar. Wolfson walked over and looked down. It was O'Malley.

"What the fuck are you bringing that in here for?" Wolfson said.

"Thought you'd want to see him, prove that he's dead," Boyle said.

His voice had a high, strained tone to it.

"Okay," Wolfson said. "He's dead. Now get him the fuck out of my saloon."

"You heard the man," Boyle said in his odd voice. "Throw him in the street in front of the Excelsior."

The two skinners dragged the body out through the rest of Boyle's mob, which came boiling in through the door.

"We wiped 'em out," Boyle said to Wolfson. "Ones ain't dead are heading for Texas."

He made a sound that might have been a giggle.

"And running hard," he said.

Wolfson nodded absently.

"We lost two hands."

"Good work, Henry," Wolfson said.

Then he turned and raised his voice to the room.

"Great work, men," he shouted. "Rest of the night, drinks on me."

The mob cheered. Wolfson looked over at me.

"Anything goes tonight, Everett," he said. "No rules. You may as well take the night off."

I nodded.

"Billie," I said. "Go to my room and go in and lock the door and don't let anybody in but me . . . or Virgil."

"I might make some money," Billie said.

"Not enough," I said. "Stay in my room. I'll take you."

She nodded. We stood and I walked with her through the saloon. Near the door to the hotel, one of Boyle's mob grabbed at Billie's arm.

"Hey, Billie, where you going," he said. "You should fuck us all."

I clubbed him across the side of the head with my fist and forearm, and he staggered back against the doorjamb, and we went out and went upstairs to my room. I took my spare handgun off the top shelf of the closet, made sure it was loaded, and put it on the nightstand.

"You know how to shoot it?" I said.

"Cock it and pull the trigger," Billie said.

"Okay," I said. "Use both hands. And don't be afraid to shoot."

"I ain't afraid to shoot," Billie said. "Anybody comes in here I'll shoot him in the pecker."

"Aim for the middle of his body," I said. "Gives you a bigger margin for error."

Billie nodded. Her eyes were very big.

"I'll wait outside until I hear the door lock," I said.

I patted her on the backside and went out. The door locked behind me, and I went on back downstairs.

# 33.

Boyle was standing on the bar, with a whiskey bottle in his left hand.

"We ain't done yet," he screamed. "Don't get drunk till we done."

The mob didn't stop drinking, but they looked at him. He pointed at the street side of the saloon.

"Across the street," he said. "Burn the Excelsior."

There was a kind of hiccup in the noise level. Then the mob cheered. "No," Wolfson shouted, but no one paid any attention.

"I want the property," Wolfson said.

"Burn it," somebody yelled. The mob took it up.

"Burn it. Burn it."

It became like a battle cry.

"No, for crissake. That's valuable property." Wolfson was screaming now, but if anyone heard him, they didn't care.

"Cato and Rose," Wolfson screamed.

The mob did hear him.

"Cato and Rose," somebody yelled.

Once again, the mob took it.

"Cato and Rose," they screamed, "Cato and Rose."

Boyle took a slug from his bottle.

"Yes," he shouted. "Yes."

"Get them," Wolfson yelled. "That'll end it."

"Drag them out of there and hang them," Boyle said.

"And don't burn the saloon," Wolfson screamed.

I walked to the back of the room where Virgil stood motionless, leaning on the back wall. My eight-gauge was leaning on the wall beside him. I picked it up.

"Cato and Rose," Boyle screamed, still standing on the bar.

"Cato and Rose," the mob answered.

"Between the mob and the booze," Virgil said to me, "Henry's 'bout as brave as he's ever gonna be."

"Think they'll do it?"

"Yep."

"I seen you face down a mob this big," I said.

"No. You seen me face down a bunch of cowboys and gun hands. This is a mob. It's killed ten, fifteen people, and it's drunk."

"Cato and Rose," Boyle screamed.

He jumped off the bar and headed for the door. The mob crowded after him. They burst out of the saloon and into the street.

"Cato and Rose," the mob chanted. "Cato and Rose."

Virgil and I walked through the suddenly empty saloon and looked out.

Across the street, in front of the Excelsior, faceup in the dirt, was O'Malley's body. Cato and Rose came out the front door of the Excelsior. Cato never took his eyes off Henry Boyle. Rose looked down at the body in the street. He smiled for a moment, nodded, and made a small, silent whistle. Then he surveyed the mob.

"We've come to hang you bastards," Boyle said.

Cato said nothing. Rose continued to survey the mob.

Then he said, "You sure you got enough?"

Virgil and I stepped out onto the porch of the Blackfoot. The mob didn't see us. It was focused on Cato and Rose.

"You won't be such a smartass cocksucker," Boyle screamed at him, "when your feet are kicking air."

Rose looked past him across the top of the mob at us standing on the porch across the narrow street.

"We gonna let this happen?" I said.

"No," Virgil said.

I nodded so that Rose could see me, and held the eight-gauge up over my head.

Rose smiled.

"I'm a talker," he said to Henry Boyle. "I'll stand out here all evening and chew the fat with you, Henry. But Cato ain't a talker. You don't get this smelly pack of vermin out of here, he'll shoot you and I'll have to start in, too."

"Like hell," Boyle yelled, and started toward the porch. The mob went with him. Cato shot Henry after he'd taken one step. Rose shot the men on either side of Boyle. Virgil shot the next one in line, and I cut loose with the eight-gauge and knocked down two people at the back. The mob turned in on itself. The eight-gauge must have sounded like a cannon from behind them. Some of the mob tried to turn toward us, some of it continued toward Cato and Rose. Some of it tried to run. We had the mob in a crossfire, and we cut it into scraps. The mob got off a few rounds, but the mob was shooting like a bunch of drunken wild men, in all directions. It hit nothing that mattered. After some frantic milling that maybe lasted a minute, the mob broke and ran, leaving Boyle and six others dead in the street with O'Malley. After they ran, there was no sound. Only the hard smell of gunpowder and some faint smoke hanging in the air. Virgil was reloading his gun. I broke the eight-gauge and put in two fresh shells. Across the way, Cato and Rose were reloading as well.

Then, in the stark silence, Cato and Rose, guns holstered, walked among the corpses across the street and joined us on the porch of the Blackfoot. Cato nodded his head once at us, and stood silent.

"Any of us get shot?" Rose said.

None of us had.

Rose said, "Thanks for the backup."

"Professional courtesy," Virgil said.

Rose nodded. Cato nodded. Both of them looked at me. I nodded.

"Lemme buy us a drink," Rose said.

"Your saloon or ours?" I said.

"We're already here," Rose said.

"We are," I said.

And we all went into the Blackfoot.

# 34.

"You saved the building," Wolfson said.

"Collative," Virgil said.

Wolfson looked at him blankly.

"Collateral," I said. "Saving the building was collateral to saving Cato and Rose."

"Oh."

"Virgil reads a lot," I said. "He got a bigger vocabulary than he knows how to use."

Virgil nodded.

We were alone in the Blackfoot, except for Wolfson and Patrick behind the bar.

"Well," Wolfson said, "whatever. I'll have the windows fixed over there by tomorrow. I'll have the sign changed and have it open and running by tomorrow night."

"Any deeds involved," Rose said. "Titles, anything?"

"Hell, no," Wolfson said. "There's a piece of property standing vacant and decrepit. A blight on the town. I'm going to rescue it, restore it, make it an asset."

"Maybe there's heirs," Virgil said.

"They show up, we'll deal with them," Wolfson said.

We all sipped a little of Wolfson's best whiskey.

"How 'bout the copper mine," I said. "If it's still worth anything."

"If it is I'll add it to Blackfoot," Wolfson said.

"What if the miners object?" I said.

Wolfson shrugged.

"How 'bout Stark?" I said. "Think he'll give you trouble."

Wolfson grinned, his loose eye wandering as he spoke.

"He won't like it when I take his lumber business," Wolfson said.

"Him, too?" I said.

"I'm going to own everything in this town," Wolfson said. "Simple as that."

"Ranches, too?" I said.

"Ranches," Wolfson said, "lumber, mining, bank, general store, saloons, hotel, everything."

Virgil was looking at Wolfson thoughtfully.

"We just shot hell out of your army," he said to Wolfson.

"Which means if I hired you four boys to help me with this," Wolfson said, "we should be pretty successful."

"What would we be doing when we weren't shooting ranchers and miners and lumberjacks?" Rose said.

"You could pretty much intimidate all those people," Wolfson said. "Don't know you'd have to do much shootin'."

"Fine," Rose said. "So what would we do otherwise?"

"Keep order," Wolfson said. "There's no law in this town. You boys could be like the law. Like Everett was in here."

"'Cept we wouldn't be the law," Virgil said.

"Be the same," Wolfson said. "'Fore you boys came here. Everett had this place turned into a damn refuge, you know? People got in trouble anywhere in town, they run here, to Everett."

"But you wasn't the law," Virgil said.

"Just in here," I said.

"Hell." Wolfson drank some more whiskey. "We be running things on this whole side of the mountain. You want laws, I'll write up some laws. You boys want to be lawmen, I'll make you lawmen."

"Just you," Virgil said.

"Boys, a town's got a right to appoint lawmen," Wolfson said. "And right now, I'm the town."

Virgil got up and walked to the saloon door and looked out at the silent street, lit by a full moon.

"Bodies are gone," he said.

"Chinamen," Wolfson said. "Take everything valuable and dump what's left outside of town. Animals eat 'em pretty clean in a couple days."

Virgil nodded slowly, staring out at the street.

"So we got a deal?" Wolfson said. "Pay you top wages."

Cato looked at Rose. I looked at both of them. None of us said anything. We all looked at Virgil, who was still staring out into the street.

Then Cato said, "What you think, Virgil?"

Virgil was silent for a moment, then, without looking back, he said, "Gotta think on it," and walked out into the moonlight.

# 35.

We could head for Texas," I said to Virgil.

"We could," Virgil said.

"I don't owe Wolfson anything," I said.

"Nope."

"You haven't even taken his money."

"True," Virgil said.

"Cato and Rose will probably stay," I said.

"Probably," Virgil said.

We were working the horses again. We'd already let them stroll. Then we'd breezed them pretty hard for a while. Now, with the reins looped over the saddle horn, we were letting them browse along, nibbling grass.

"We could head for Texas," I said.

"Could," Virgil said.

"Ain't we just had this talk?" I said.

"Yep."

"So why don't we head for Texas," I said.

"Ain't time yet," Virgil said.

"Because?"

Virgil leaned back in his saddle and looked up at an eagle circling slow and easy on the air currents in the sky.

"Don't want Wolfson running the town," Virgil said.

"Why not?"

"Same reason we didn't want that mob lynching Cato and Rose," Virgil said.

"'Cause it would be against the law?"

Virgil shook his head. The horses moseyed along, reins loose, head down, nosing at the grass.

"I ain't a lawman," he said.

"Good thing," I said. "Ain't nothing happened here since I got here had anything to do with law."

"Had to do with us shooting better than them," Virgil said.

"It did," I said.

"Better than shootin' worse," Virgil said.

There was a stream to the right. In the late summer it would probably be dry. But for now, it came up near the bottom of the hills behind us and found its way down a shallow wash to the bigger stream that ran among the homestead ranches. The horses smelled it and veered over to it and drank from it. Virgil patted his horse's neck quietly while he drank.

"Don't feel bad about anything I done here," I said.

Virgil patted his horse some more. He nodded.

"I know," he said.

You got any money left?" I said.

"Not much," Virgil said.

"Me either."

"Don't need much," Virgil said.

"Got to have some," I said.

"Maybe we should work for Wolfson," Virgil said. "While we see how things develop."

"And if they develop wrong?"

"Don't know about wrong," Virgil said. "But Wolfson shouldn't run the whole town."

"With Cato and Rose to back him."

"So if it goes that way, we quit?"

"Probably," Virgil said.

"And do what?" I said.

"Can't say."

"Might have to go against Cato and Rose," I said.

"Might."

"And you're willing?"

"Yep."

"Yesterday you was saving their lives," I said.

"We was," Virgil said.

"What's the difference?"

"Don't know," Virgil said. "Maybe we'll find out."

We picked up our reins and lifted the horses' heads and pointed them back toward town.

"Virgil," I said as the horses walked toward home, "I get killed while you figure out what you are, I'm gonna resent it."

Virgil nodded.

"Don't blame you," he said.

# 36.

So we were all working for Wolfson. Me and Virgil doing lookout duty at the Blackfoot. Cato and Rose doing the same at the Excelsior. It was a lot more firepower than either saloon needed. And we all knew it. But we also all knew that keeping order in a couple of saloons was not why Wolfson paid us. It was just something useful to do while we waited.

On a wet Tuesday morning Virgil and I, with our hats pulled down and our collars turned up, rode through the hard rain, up to the copper mine with Wolfson.

"We couldn't do this tomorrow?" I said to Wolfson.

"Decided to do it today," Wolfson said. "Gonna do it today. When I do business, I do business."

Wolfson looked sort of funny on horseback, out in the daylight. He had on a black slicker and a big hat, and seemed out of place.

"Fine," I said.

Virgil said nothing. I knew he could barely tolerate Wolfson.

At the mine we put the horses under a tarpaulin shelter beside the mine shack and went on and had some coffee with the mine foreman, a tall, stoop-shouldered guy with a lot of gray beard. His name, he said, was Faison.

"Sorry about the trouble up here last week," Wolfson said. "I hope no miners were hurt."

"Nope, we stayed low," Faison said.

"Smart," Wolfson said.

"You taking over the mine?" Faison said.

"I'd like to do that," Wolfson said. "Keep everybody on, promote you to mine manager."

"More money?" Faison said.

"Of course," Wolfson said.

Faison nodded.

"Nobody misses O'Malley," Faison said. "Or the gun hands he brought in, neither."

He looked at Virgil and me.

"No offense," he said.

I shook my head. Virgil said nothing.

"Only thing anybody misses is payday," Faison said. "You keep the paydays in order, we'll be happy to work for you."

"Excellent," Wolfson said. "You bring the books into

town soon as you can, go over them with Hensdale, my chief clerk, at the emporium."

"I know Hensdale," Faison said.

"Good." Wolfson raised his coffee cup. "Here's to bigger and better paydays."

Faison nodded and raised his cup. Virgil and I did nothing. Wolfson might have glanced at us. It was always hard to tell because of the random eye.

"One favor," Wolfson said after he'd put his cup back down. "I'd like a new sign that says *Wolfson Mining.*"

"Sure," Faison said.

He and Wolfson shook hands, and we left. It was still raining steady, and the horses were not happy to leave the shelter of the tarpaulin.

"We going to talk with Stark?" I said.

"Wolfson said we were."

"I wouldn't expect much from Stark," I said.

"Fritzie is smart," Wolfson said. "He's a businessman. He sees how the landscape has changed."

I glanced at Virgil. He shrugged. The rain slanted in on us riding east. Virgil rode the same way as he did when it was sunny or cold or windy or not. Things didn't make much impression on Virgil Cole. He just went on being Virgil Cole . . . except about Allie. We rode across the face of the hill for an hour to Stark's lumber operation. The rain didn't encourage talking. We left the horses under cover in a lumber shed and went to the office. Stark let us in.

"What the hell do you want, Wolfson?" Stark said.

"Just stopping by, say hello, talk about how things have changed."

"I got no interest in talking with you," Stark said. "And I don't care what's changed and what hasn't."

"I thought maybe we should talk about partnering up."

"Partnering up?" Stark said. "With you?"

"Fritzie, look around," Wolfson said. "I got this whole town, hell, the whole west slope, tied up pretty tight. It's to your fucking benefit, you know? To partner with me."

"Wolfson," Stark said, "you are a greedy, slimy, pig-fucking sonovabitch. I wouldn't partner with you in Paradise. You're a thief. You're a back shooter. You're a fucking coward hiding behind vermin like these two."

"You better think about what you're saying," Wolfson said.

"I've thought all I want to about it, you walleyed cock-sucker," Stark said. "I ain't afraid of you or your two gunners, neither."

"Maybe you'll learn to be," Wolfson said.

"And maybe I won't," Stark said.

He picked up an ax handle that lay on his desk.

"So unless you're ready to fucking shoot me now," he said, "get out of my office and off my land."

Wolfson stared at him. Stark took a step toward him with the ax handle raised. Wolfson took a quick back step.

"No," he said. "We won't shoot you today."

"Then get your ass out of here," Stark said.

"But there's no guarantees about another day," Wolfson said. "Think on it."

"Fuck you," Stark said.

An argument like that doesn't leave you with much to say. Wolfson turned and strode out of the lumber office. Virgil grinned at Stark for a moment, then we went after Wolfson. When we were on our mounts and heading back toward town, nobody said anything.

Finally, Virgil looked at me with the same grin he'd given Stark.

"Vermin," he said.

# 37.

We were having a drink before work with Cato and Rose in the Blackfoot. A good-looking woman came in from the hotel lobby. She was wearing a blue gingham dress and a ribbon in her hair. She saw the four of us at the bar and walked over.

"I need help," she said.

"Ladies don't usually come in here," I said.

"I don't care," she said. "It's worse out there."

She had a purple bruise on her left cheekbone that had begun to turn yellow, which meant she'd had it for a while. She'd probably made the dress herself, but it fit pretty well. Her dark hair looked as if she brushed it a lot. She seemed well-scrubbed.

"What do you need," I said.

"My husband just hit me in the stomach and knocked me down."

"Doesn't look like the first time," I said.

"No."

"What's different about this time," I said.

"He was kicking me."

"Where'd this happen," I said.

"In the emporium."

"And you got away from him and ran in here?"

"Yes," she said. "But he'll be in here after me."

"What's holding him up?" I said.

"He's got to get the children into the wagon," she said.

We all looked at her, even Cato.

"The children," I said.

"He beats me up in front of them all the time," she said.

Her voice was steady. But I could see that her hands were shaking.

"What's your name," I said.

"Beth," she said. "Beth Redmond."

"Bob Redmond's wife?" I said.

"Yes."

The saloon doors on the street side swung open and Redmond pushed in.

"Speak of the devil," I said.

"Beth," Redmond said when he saw her standing with us. "What are you, a goddamned whore? Get out of this place."

She didn't move.

"You hear me, woman?" Redmond said. "Out! Now!"

Cato Tillson looked at Mrs. Redmond and said, "You want me to kill him?"

"Kill him?" Mrs. Redmond said.

"Yes."

"I . . . no," she said. "God, no."

"Okay," Cato said.

He picked up his drink and leaned back in his chair to watch. For the first time, I think, it registered to Redmond who we were. He didn't like it. But he had to be forceful. His wife was watching.

"This is none of your business," he said. "Any of you."

None of us said anything.

"I don't know what she told you; she's a lying bitch anyway. But I can't have my wife flaunting herself like a floozy in a saloon."

None of us said anything.

"So you either come right now, bitch," he said to his wife, "or I'll come over and drag you out by the hair of your head."

None of us said anything. But Virgil stepped away from the bar and moved over to stand in front of Mrs. Redmond.

Redmond paused.

"This is family business," he said.

Virgil said nothing.

Redmond looked at the rest of us.

"It is, you know," he said. "Nobody got the right to interfere between a man and his wife."

None of us said anything. Redmond looked at his wife again.

"What kind of whore are you, hiding from your husband behind this . . . this fucking . . . fucking gun shooter?"

Behind Virgil, Mrs. Redmond shook her head but didn't say anything. Nobody else said anything. Nobody moved. Redmond didn't have a gun. His good luck. If he'd had one he might have tried to use it. Bad luck, though, for Mrs. Redmond. If he tried to shoot with Virgil, he'd be dead and she'd be free of him.

"Okay," he said. "Okay. That's how it is, whore. Just don't think you can come home after this."

"I can't come with you, Bob," Mrs. Redmond said. "I can't anymore."

"Just stay away from me and my children," he said.

She opened her mouth and took a short breath, and didn't speak. He looked at her and turned his head and spit on the floor. He was careful, I noticed, not to spit on Virgil. Then he turned stiffly and marched out.

"Oh my God," Mrs. Redmond said. "Oh my God!"

She began to cry.

# 38.

We got her to a table, and she sat down.

"Do you drink whiskey?" Virgil said.

She nodded as she cried. I gestured to Patrick and he brought us a good-sized glass of whiskey.

"Wolfson's," Patrick said as he put the glass down.

Mrs. Redmond picked it up with both hands and tried to hold the crying long enough to drink some. Breathing in tiny, shallow breaths, she managed to take a slug and swallow it. Then she put the glass down and cried some more.

After a while she took another slug and said, "What am I going to do?"

"What do you need?" Virgil said.

"I have no money, no clothes, no place to stay, nowhere to go," she said.

"You can stay here," Virgil said.

"Here?"

"In the hotel," Virgil said.

"But I can't pay."

"We'll arrange something," I said. "Room at the hotel, meals, charge what you need at the emporium."

"But . . ." She didn't quite know how to ask the question. She drank some whiskey.

"But do I have to . . . do I have to do anything?" she said.

Virgil smiled.

"No," he said. "You don't."

Wolfson came into the saloon through the door that connected to the hotel lobby, and walked straight to our table.

"What the hell is she doing here," he said.

"Having a drink," Virgil said. "With me."

It was a simple answer. But there was something in it that made Wolfson rein in.

"Well, I see that, Virgil," Wolfson said. "But we don't normally see women like her in here. She ain't a whore, is she?"

"No," Virgil said.

"No offense, ma'am," Wolfson said.

Mrs. Redmond shook her head. She was beginning to enjoy the whiskey.

"I'd like her to be a guest of the Blackfoot," Virgil said. "Room, board, charge what she needs at the emporium."

"Sure," Wolfson said. "Who pays."

"She doesn't," Virgil said.

"So who pays?" Wolfson said.

"We was thinking it would be you, Amos," I said. "You know, guest of the Blackfoot?"

"Including the emporium?" Wolfson said. "Why the fuck would I do that?"

Frank Rose was sitting with his elbows on the table, and his chin resting on his folded hands. He winked at Mrs. Redmond.

"Harmonious relationship," he said to Wolfson, "with your gun hands."

"What the fuck does that mean?" Wolfson said.

"Can't speak for Cole and Hitch," Rose said. "But me and Cato will quit if she don't get what she needs."

"Quit?"

I looked at Virgil and nodded.

"That would be the occasion," Virgil said, "among me and Everett, too."

"And some of us might be kind of mad about it," Rose said.

Cato stared straight at Wolfson and nodded his head slowly.

"You are threatening me," Wolfson said.

Rose grinned at him.

"Only a little," Rose said.

"Are you saying that if I don't give this fucking woman room, board, and emporium charge privileges, you'll quit?"

Rose looked at Cato, then at Virgil and me. All three of us nodded.

"Yes," Rose said. "That's pretty much it."

"And you might cause trouble?" Wolfson said.

"We're pretty good at that," Rose said.

"For crissake," Wolfson said. "Is she doing all of you?"

"None of us," Virgil said. "And clean up your talk."

Wolfson started to say something. Virgil was looking at him steadily.

"Room, board, free stuff at the store," Wolfson said.

Virgil nodded. Wolfson looked at Mrs. Redmond.

He said, "You got anything to add, lady?"

"Her name is Mrs. Redmond," Virgil said.

"Beth," she said. "Beth Redmond."

"You're Bob Redmond's wife?"

She nodded.

"Jesus Christ," Wolfson said.

He turned away from the table.

"You'll arrange it?" I said.

"Oh, fuck," Wolfson said, and kept walking. "I'll arrange it."

# 39.

Patrick brought the bottle over and poured us all another drink. Mrs. Redmond took a drink and stared into her glass. She had stopped crying. And she was a little drunk.

"He isn't as bad a man as he seems," she said.

"Hard to be worse," I said.

"He is just so strained," she said, "trying to support me and the kids, and trying to organize the ranchers, and trying to fight Mr. Wolfson."

None of us said anything.

"He gets crazy mad, sometimes," she said.

"At you," I said.

She nodded.

"But he never hurts the kids," she said.

"He ain't supposed to," Virgil said.

She stared at him. I knew she didn't understand him. Most people didn't. There was about him a flat deadliness that frightened people. And yet he had protected her from her husband and helped her get settled in the Blackfoot.

"He wasn't always like this," she said. "It's just that all we got is that piece of land, and he's terrified we're going to lose it. That Mr. Wolfson will take it away from us."

"Make him feel like a failure," I said.

"Yes."

"This ain't gonna help him," Virgil said. "Us taking his wife away from him."

"You didn't do that," she said.

"He'll see it that way," Virgil said.

Virgil probably knew something about that feeling. Mrs. Redmond drank more whiskey and began to cry again. She talked haltingly while she cried.

"My children." She gasped. "My children. He won't let me see my children."

"He might," Virgil said.

She shook her head.

"His mind is set," she said. "When he sets it, ain't nothing will change it."

"Couple of us could take you out for a visit," Virgil said.

She shook her head.

"No," she said. "There might be trouble. I wouldn't want the children to see it."

"Well, then," Virgil said. "Maybe Everett and me can ride out tomorrow and talk with him about this."

"Oh, God," she said. "Not in front of the children."

"They home all the time?"

"They go a couple hours in the afternoon to Ruth Anne Markey, Charlie Markey's wife. She teaches some of the kids in her home. Mostly Bob needs them to help with the place."

"We can do it then," Virgil said.

She stared at him again.

"Don't hurt him," she said. "Please don't hurt him."

"'Course not," Virgil said.

Mrs. Redmond was silent for a time, staring into her glass. Then she pushed the glass away, folded her arms on the tabletop, and put her head down on her arms. In a few moments she was snoring softly.

"Care to give me a hand, Everett," Virgil said.

I nodded, and we stood, and each with a hand under her arm, we got her to her feet and steered her to her hotel room.

# 40.

The horses had been ridden together so often that, both geldings, they had become friends. They would occasionally nuzzle each other when we stopped.

"Isn't this sort of the way you took up with Allie?" I said to Virgil.

"How so?" Virgil said.

"She comes into town alone. No money. No place to stay. You find her a place to stay. Get her a job."

"Uh-huh."

"How'd that work out for you?" I said.

"Don't know yet," Virgil said.

"Damn," I said. "You are a stubborn bastard."

"I am," Virgil said.

The horses moved along pleasantly. The air was warm,

not hot, and there was a nice little breeze. Virgil rode well. He did everything well. When he rode, the horse seemed an extension of him. When he shot, the gun seemed part of him.

"Hard on women out here," Virgil said.

"Hard on everybody out here," I said.

"Women need looking after."

"Allie?" I said. "I figure Allie's pretty good at taking care of herself."

"Allie thinks with her twat," Virgil said. "It gets her in trouble."

"True," I said. "So what are you going to do with Mrs. Redmond?"

"Don't know," Virgil said. "Can't let her old man beat on her."

"We could let Cato kill him," I said.

"Can't do that," Virgil said.

"Why not?" I said.

"Can't do that," Virgil said, as if it was an answer.

The horses eased down the trail toward the homesteads on the flat land. The homesteads weren't much. Weather-grayed cabin and shed. Sparse-looking kitchen garden. An occasional split-rail corral with one or two horses. Redmond's was no different. We found him straddling the peak of his cabin, patching the roof. When he saw us ride in he climbed down and went inside. By the time we reached the house, he was back outside with a Winchester.

"What do you want?" he said.

"Need to talk," Virgil said.

"Got nothing to talk about," Redmond said.

"You do," Virgil said.

Redmond gestured with the Winchester.

"I know how to use this," he said.

"'Course you do," Virgil said. "You might get off a shot. You might even hit one of us. But 'fore you jacked the second shell up into the chamber you'd be dead."

"And maybe one of you'd be dead."

"Maybe," Virgil said.

There was some silence. Virgil's horse put his head over and snuffled at mine. Redmond lowered the Winchester slightly.

"What you want to talk about?" he said.

"Your wife and children," Virgil said.

"Goddamn it," Redmond said. "Wolfson don't run my family."

"This ain't Wolfson," Virgil said. "This is me."

He was relaxed and comfortable in his saddle as he talked. Like he always was. Sometimes people would make a bad mistake and think he wasn't ready. He was. Virgil was always ready. He just never looked it.

"You fucking her yet?" Redmond said.

"Nope."

"Probably all of you, fucking her," Redmond said.

"Nope."

"Well, I'll give her that," Redmond said. "She's hot enough. Or she used to be."

"That be before you starting smacking her around?" Virgil said.

"That's none of your business," Redmond said.

"True enough," Virgil said. "But she needs to see the kids."

"She can't," Redmond said.

"Me and Everett," Virgil said, "think she should visit the children, couple times a week. Cato and Rose agree with us."

"You threatenin' me?" Redmond said.

"I am," Virgil said.

Again, silence. Redmond and Virgil looked at each other. Nobody could hold a stare very long with Virgil Cole. Redmond looked away.

"What if I say no?"

"Four of us will bring her out anyway," Virgil said.

"Four fucking pistoleros against one farmer?" Redmond said.

"Yup."

"Don't seem fair," Redmond said.

"One of us comes out," Virgil said. "And you might try to shoot it out, and whoever would have to kill you. Four of us come out, and you won't be that stupid."

Redmond looked at Virgil. Then at me. I smiled at him. He looked back at Virgil.

"I already told them she's a whore," Redmond said.

"Tell 'em she ain't," Virgil said.

My horse tossed his head, and the sound of the bridle hardware was the only sound.

"Kids should probably see their mother," Redmond said.

"Should," Virgil said.

"When you want to bring her out?" Redmond said finally.

"Monday and Friday," Virgil said.

Redmond nodded.

"Lunchtime," Redmond said.

"Okay."

"Don't need all four of you to come."

"Maybe at first," Virgil said. "See how it goes."

Redmond thought about it awhile.

"Why do you people give a fuck about me and Beth?" he said.

"Good to keep busy," Virgil said.

Redmond nodded slowly. More to himself, I think, than to us.

"Four killers," he said. "Four fucking gun-shooting killers."

Virgil nodded.

"And all of a sudden," Redmond said, "you're like fucking law and order, for crissake."

"Peculiar, ain't it," Virgil said.

# 41.

With Cato and Rose at the Excelsior, and me and Virgil at the Blackfoot, things got so peaceful that I stopped sitting in the lookout chair and sat with Virgil at a table near the bar.

"Quiet," I said to Virgil.

"It is," he said.

"Makes you wonder if they need us here," I said.

"They'd need us if we wasn't here," Virgil said.

"Same at the Excelsior," I said.

"Should be," Virgil said.

"Cute," I said. "They don't need us unless we ain't here; then they do need us."

"Called keepin' the peace," Virgil said.

"That'd be us," I said.

Two farmers came into the Blackfoot, and looked around, and came to our table.

One of them, a short, chunky guy wearing a pink shirt, said, "Cole and Hitch?"

"He's Cole," I said. "I'm Hitch."

"We got a problem," the farmer in the pink shirt said.

The man with him was taller and rounder. He was wearing a blue shirt.

"He's got a problem," the man in blue said. "Sonovabitch sold me a lame horse."

"He had a chance to try the horse," Pink Shirt said. "He didn't say nothing about her bein' lame when he bought her."

"How lame," Virgil said.

"Lame," Blue Shirt said, "right front leg's all swole."

"Why?"

They both looked at him blankly.

"Why's it swole?" Virgil said.

"'Cause she's lame," Blue Shirt said.

"Wasn't swole when I sold her," Pink Shirt said.

Virgil took a long breath through his nose.

"Where's the horse," Virgil said.

"Out front," Blue Shirt said.

"Lemme see her," Virgil said.

He and I stood, and all of us went outside.

The horse was a sorrel mare and pretty long in the tooth. Virgil sat on his haunches beside her, and looked at her swollen right foreleg without touching it. He nodded to himself.

"Everett," he said. "Get me a bottle of good whiskey and a clean cloth."

I went in and got what he ordered and came out with it.

"Gashed her leg on something," Virgil said. "It's infected."

I handed him the cloth and the whiskey.

"Take her head," Virgil said. "I'm gonna clean her wound."

I held the horse by the bridle straps. Virgil carefully picked up her foreleg and held it between his legs, his back to the horse.

"Hang on," Virgil said.

I put my weight on the head straps.

"Easy, darlin'," Virgil said to the horse. Virgil poured about half the whiskey into a gash on her foreleg. The horse lunged back. I held her head. Virgil rode her foreleg comfortably, murmuring to the horse all the time, and in a moment she stopped lunging. He studied the gash.

"Again," he said.

I clamped on the harness, and he clamped the foreleg tight between his legs and poured the rest of the whiskey over her wound. She struggled long this time, but we rode it out and she calmed down again. Virgil tore the cloth into strips and bandaged the wound. He continued to murmur to the horse as he had since he started. The horse stayed docile. Virgil stood.

"Whiskey ought to kill the infection," he said. "Change the bandage every day. Week or so she'll be fine."

"I don't want no damaged horse," Blue Shirt said.

"Well, you bought her," Pink Shirt said.

Virgil was standing next to the horse, patting her absently on the shoulder.

"Either she had the gash when you bought her," Virgil said, "and you were too stupid to see it, or you caused the gash after you bought her and were too stupid to treat it."

"You're saying it's my fault."

"I'm saying you take care of the horse, and in a couple weeks she'll be fine."

"I'm not taking care of this damn horse," Blue Shirt said.

"You are," Virgil said.

Blue Shirt stared at him. Virgil looked at him steadily.

"What if I don't?" Blue Shirt said.

"I'll kill you," Virgil said.

"Kill me?"

"Yep."

"Over this fleabag of a fucking horse?" Blue Shirt said.

"Yep."

"So," Pink Shirt said. "It's settled then."

Virgil turned his head slowly and looked at Pink Shirt.

"Put her in the livery stable," Virgil said. "You pay."

"That's not fair."

"It's how it is," Virgil said. "Me and Everett will be checking. Anything happens to the horse, you answer to us."

Blue Shirt took the lead from the hitching post and began to walk the horse slowly down the main street toward the livery stable.

"How 'bout we split the cost of the livery?" Pink Shirt said.

"Fuck you," Blue Shirt said.

They kept walking and they didn't look back. Virgil and I went back into the Blackfoot.

"Sheriff, judge, and jury," I said.

Virgil grinned at me and said, "Got nothing else to do."

# 42.

We rented Mrs. Redmond a buggy at the livery stable and rode out with her to her husband's ranch. A hundred yards or so upslope from the ranch we stopped.

"You go on down," Virgil said.

She didn't say anything, but her face was tight and there was no color in it.

"Go ahead," Virgil said. "We'll be right here."

She chucked to the horse and slapped the reins and the buggy went on down the easy slope to the ranch. As she got there the kids came out of the house and stood on the front porch. When the buggy stopped, the kids stared at their mother without moving. She said something to them, and after a moment they climbed into the buggy. The four of us sat our horses in a row on the hillside and watched. Rose on the left, Cato next to him, me, and Virgil on the right. Redmond never showed himself.

Mrs. Redmond sat in the buggy with her children for maybe an hour. The four of us sat our horses on the slope and watched. Then the kids climbed down and went to stand on the porch. The buggy turned slowly and started back up the slope. The kids watched as it went. When it reached us, she was crying.

"They want to know when I'm coming home," she said. "They want to know when I'm going to stop being bad. They want to know if I'm mad at them. They want to know if Daddy is mad at me."

Nobody said anything. We wheeled our horses in behind the buggy and rode in silence back to town.

"How's that mare doing," Virgil said to the stableman while he helped Mrs. Redmond down from the carriage.

"Good, Mr. Cole. Swelling's way down."

"Keep an eye on her," Virgil said.

"You bet, Mr. Cole."

We delivered Mrs. Redmond to her hotel room and then went into the saloon. Wolfson was waiting for us.

"Well, here it is," Wolfson said. "The fucking pistolero benevolent society. I hire you to take care of beat-up women and old nags, for crissake?"

"You hire us to keep the peace for you," Rose said.

He spread his hands to encompass the saloon and the street in front of it.

"Look how peaceful," he said.

Wolfson nodded.

"Yeah, yeah," he said. "I know. But sometimes I'm not so sure whether you work for me or I work for you."

"We're in this together, Amos," Virgil said. "We all got collaborative goals."

"'Less I don't pay you," Wolfson said.

"That might change things," Rose said. "Right, Cato?"

"Sure," Cato said.

"Well if you ain't too busy with your fucking charity work," Wolfson said, "maybe you'll be good enough to ride out with me in the morning and foreclose on a bean wrangler."

"Can't pay his bill?" Virgil said.

"That's right, so I'm taking his ranch in lieu."

"Anybody we know?" I said.

"It ain't Redmond, if that's what you're asking."

"That's what I was asking," I said.

# 43.

We rode out the next morning, past Redmond's ranch, farther out along the creek, with the warm morning sun on our backs. Wolfson was with us, and his chief clerk, Hensdale. Hensdale didn't seem too happy being out where Wolfson actually did a lot of his business.

"There's any trouble, Hen," Wolfson said to him, "these boys will take care of it."

"So why do I even have to come along?" Hensdale said.

"Because I fucking want you along," Wolfson said. "You understand that?"

"Yes, sir," Hensdale said.

"Good," Wolfson said. "What's this fella's name again?"

"Ward," Hensdale said. "Stanton Ward."

The creek curved a little west and straightened out again,

flowing south, and in the bend was the Ward ranch. It wasn't much, less than Redmond's. But the land was good, right by the creek. In front of the house there were twelve farmers, many of them with Winchesters or shotguns.

"Jesus," Hensdale murmured.

We rode in and stopped in front of the farmers. One of them was Redmond. He had his Winchester.

"Don't shoot Redmond," Virgil said.

Cato and Rose both nodded. I nodded,

Wolfson said, "What the hell?"

Virgil paid him no mind. Cato and Rose fanned out to the right.

"There's any shooting," I said to Hensdale, "lie flat over your horse's neck and get the hell out of here."

Hensdale nodded. Virgil and I fanned left. We left Wolfson in the center, in front of Redmond, with Hensdale unhappily beside him. I could see Virgil studying the ranchers on our side of the action, deciding who to shoot first. On the other side of Wolfson, I could see Cato Tillson doing the same thing.

"Fella with the straw hat first," Virgil said. "Then the one with the blue striped shirt."

I nodded. I didn't know how Virgil decided these things, but he had a way, and I trusted it. I rested the eight-gauge across my saddle.

"Ward?" Wolfson said.

A short, round man with a sandy beard was standing beside Redmond.

"I'm Ward," he said.

"You owe me money," Wolfson said.

Ward didn't answer.

"How much?" Wolfson said to Hensdale.

Hensdale gave the figure in a soft voice, meant to suggest that it wasn't his fault, he was only the bean counter.

"You got it?" Wolfson said.

"How's he gonna have it," Redmond said.

He was talking to Wolfson, but I knew he was aware of Virgil.

"Not my problem, you owe me, you can't pay. I collect my collateral."

"For God's sake, Wolfson," Redmond said. "Man's got four children."

"Didn't come here to argue," Wolfson said. "If I had, I wouldn'ta brought my friends."

He nodded in a way to include the four of us.

"We ain't gonna let you take his house," Redmond said.

"That the way you see it, Ward?" Wolfson said.

Ward's eyes shifted from Virgil to Cato Tillson to Rose and to me. Then he looked back at Wolfson.

"I . . . I can't pay you," he said. "Maybe if you gimme time."

Wolfson shook his head.

"Time's up," he said. "We'll wait here while you pack up the family and go."

"He ain't going," Redmond said.

Virgil nudged his horse forward at a slow pace and rode him gently between Redmond and Ward. Then he moved the horse sidestep and eased Redmond slowly away from Ward.

On the other side of Ward, Cato did the same thing to the farmer on that side. Rose and I followed and eased the next couple of clodhoppers away from Ward, and from each other.

"Don't let them move us," Redmond shouted, and tried to step around Virgil. Virgil herded him with his horse, like he was cutting out a steer.

"Hold it," Redmond shouted. "Hold it or we'll start shooting."

"No," Ward screamed. "No. I don't want the fucking property."

Virgil stopped his horse and sat still. The rest of us did the same.

"I can't live like this," Ward said. "I can't live here waiting for the next shootout. I'm a rancher. I don't want this."

No one moved.

Then Redmond said, "Stan, if we don't stop him here, where will we stop him?"

"Don't care," Ward said. "Stop him without me. Ranch is yours, Wolfson. I'll take the horses, the wagon, and whatever we can load on it. Rest is yours."

"Wise choice," Wolfson said. "We'll wait."

Slowly, watching Redmond as he did, Virgil backed his horse up. The rest of us did the same. Redmond half-raised his Winchester. Virgil had no reaction. The hammer was down on the Winchester. Meant that Redmond would either have to work the lever or cock it, and that, for Virgil, was an ocean of time.

"Disagreement's been revolved," Virgil said. "Time to go home."

The man in the straw hat said to Ward, "Need a hand with the wagon?"

Ward nodded.

"'Preciate it, Saul," he said.

They turned and went toward the house. Some of the others went with them; the rest began to drift toward their horses.

"It'll happen to one of us next, and then another one," Redmond said in a high voice, "and another one, until he's got it all."

The rancher in the blue striped shirt paused near his horse. He was carrying his Winchester with the barrel pointing toward the ground.

He said to Redmond, "We ain't gunmen, Bob."

Then he swung up into the saddle and rode away.

# 44.

Virgil and I were leaning on the bar, watching the smoke swirl and the whiskey pour and the cards slap down on tabletops.

"Spent a lot of my life in saloons like this," Virgil said.

"I know," I said.

"Funny thing is, neither one of us drinks much."

"Probably a good thing," I said.

"Probably," Virgil said.

He looked comfortably around, appearing to pay no attention, in fact seeing everything.

"I been reading a book by this guy Russo," Virgil said.

"Who?"

"French guy, Russo. Wrote something called *The Social Contract*, lot of stuff about nature."

"Rousseau," I said.

"Yeah, him," Virgil said.

Virgil never admitted to a mistake. But if he was corrected, he never made it again.

"He says that men are good, and what makes them bad is government and law and stuff."

"Don't know much about Rousseau," I said.

"Didn't teach you 'bout him?" Virgil said. "At the Point?"

"Nope. Spent a lot of time on Roman cavalry tactics," I said. "Not so much on French philosophers."

"That what he was?" Virgil said. "A philosopher?"

"I think so," I said.

"Well, he says if people was just left to grow up natural, they'd be good," Virgil said. "You think that's so?"

"Don't know," I said. "And I ain't so sure it matters."

Virgil nodded.

"'Cause nobody ever grew up that way," he said.

I nodded.

"And probably ain't going to," Virgil said.

I nodded again.

"So what difference does it make?" I said.

"I dunno," Virgil said. "I like reading about it. I like to learn stuff."

"Sure," I said.

"And if this Rousseau is right, then the law ain't a good thing, that protects people; it's a bad thing that, like, makes them bad."

"Ain't much law here," I said.

"'Cept us," Virgil said.

I laughed.

"'Cept us," I said.

Virgil grinned.

"And Cato and Rose," he said.

We both laughed.

"There's some law for you," I said.

"And it don't much come from no government," Virgil said, "or any, you know, contract or nothing."

"Nope," I said.

"Comes 'cause we can shoot better than other people."

"And ain't afraid to," I said.

Wolfson came across the room and stopped in front of us.

"Virgil," he said. "I got something to say."

Virgil nodded.

"I mean alone," Wolfson said.

"Go ahead and talk in front of Everett," Virgil said. "Save me the trouble of telling him what you said."

Wolfson didn't like it, but Virgil showed no sign that he cared.

"I didn't appreciate you telling people not to shoot Redmond," Wolfson said.

"You wanted him shot?" Virgil said.

"I want to decide those things, not you."

"Don't blame you," Virgil said. "But you ain't doing the shooting."

Wolfson frowned.

"I don't get you, Cole," he said. "I'd expect that you'd want him dead."

"Why's that?"

"Well," Wolfson said, "I mean, you're fucking his wife."

Virgil stared at Wolfson and said nothing.

"Well, I mean, no offense," Wolfson said.

Virgil stared silently.

"Damn it, Cole, you work for me, don't you?" Wolfson said. "You act like you're in charge of everything. Like you don't work for anybody."

Virgil shrugged. Wolfson looked at me.

"You too, Everett," he said. "You act like a couple fucking English kings, you know? Like you can do what you want."

"And Cato and Rose ain't much better," I said.

"No, goddamn it, they ain't," Wolfson said.

"You ever read Rousseau?" Virgil said.

"I don't read shit," Wolfson said. "Including Roo whatever his fucking name is."

"Nope," Virgil said. "'Spect you haven't."

He turned and spoke to Patrick.

"I'd like just a finger of whiskey," he said.

Patrick poured some, and a shot for me as well. He held the bottle up toward Wolfson, and Wolfson shook his head.

"Things gonna have to change around here," he said, and turned and walked away.

"Things gonna change," he muttered as he walked. "Things gonna fucking change."

"Why doesn't he fire us?" I said.

"He's scared of us," Virgil said.

"And Cato and Rose," I said.

"Same thing," he said.

"So what do you think he'll do?"

"Hire himself enough people to back him," Virgil said. "Then he'll feel safe. Then he'll fire us."

"You and me."

"Uh-huh."

"Cato and Rose?"

"Uh-huh."

We sipped our whiskey.

After a while I said to Virgil, "Is it true?"

"What?"

"What he said. You poking Mrs. Redmond?"

"Ain't gentlemanly to tell," Virgil said.

I nodded.

"Hell, it ain't even too gentlemanly to ask," Virgil said.

"You are," I said.

Virgil shrugged.

"Well," I said, "ain't you some kind of dandy."

"Always have been," Virgil said.

# 45.

The next time we took Mrs. Redmond out to the ranch, Redmond came out of the house with the children and Mrs. Redmond climbed down from the buggy and went and sat on the porch with them while we sat our horses up the slope a ways.

"You pay any of Wolfson's whores, Everett?" Frank Rose said.

I nodded.

"They're all Wolfson's whores," I said.

"He says we can use anyone we want, no charge," Rose said. "And a whore wants to give it to me for nothing, I'll take it, and so will Cato. But me and Cato, we figure it ain't Wolfson's to say, you know? I mean, he don't quite own 'em.

Unless we pay them when they fuck us, they're getting nothing."

Rose grinned.

"'Cept a'course the ride of a lifetime. How 'bout you, Virgil? You agree with that."

"Uh-huh."

"Cole don't need no whores," Cato said.

All three of us looked at him. Cato was still looking downhill at the Redmond ranch. Rose looked at Virgil, then suddenly down the hill at Beth Redmond. Then back at Virgil.

"Mrs. Redmond," he said.

Virgil said nothing. Neither did Cato.

Rose looked at me. I shrugged.

We all looked down the hill, and no one spoke for a time.

Then Rose said, "Any one of us can deal with Redmond. Ain't this a waste of manpower or something?"

"Maybe he don't know that," Virgil said.

"You mean if only one of us comes with her," Rose said, "he might be tempted to give it a try?"

"Maybe."

"And you don't want him to get hurt."

"Nope."

"'Cause of the wife."

"Maybe."

"Ain't got much use for a man beats on women," Rose said. "You, Cato?"

"No," Cato said.

"Not much of a man," Rose said.

"No," Cato said.

"He's the only one fighting Wolfson," I said.

"And he ain't winning," Rose said.

"True," I said.

"You'd think Wolfson would be happy," Rose said.

"But he's not."

"Hell, no," Rose said. "He talked to me and Cato about you and Virgil. He don't seem happy with Virgil."

"Talked to you 'bout backing him," Virgil said. "If he fired us."

"Said he couldn't trust you to do what he told you," Rose said.

Virgil smiled.

"Tole him he could trust you to do what you said you would," Rose said.

"That's true," Virgil said. "You tell him you'd back him?"

"No," Rose said. "Tole him we wouldn't."

# 46.

You went out to the Ward ranch the other day," Mrs. Redmond said.

"We did," Virgil said.

The three of us were having our coffee on the front porch of the hotel, watching the soft rain thicken the street dust into mud.

"My husband was there," she said.

"Yep."

"Mr. Rose says you told everybody not to hurt him," she said.

"Mr. Rose is a talker," Virgil said.

"But you did say that."

"Something like that," Virgil said.

"He told us, 'Don't shoot Redmond,'" I said.

"Did you do that for me?" Mrs. Redmond said.

"Yes," Virgil said.

She was quiet for a time, holding the thick mug in both hands.

"He's not a bad man," she said after a while.

Virgil didn't say anything.

"Good men don't generally beat up their women," I said.

She drank some more coffee.

"I know," she said. "But . . ."

There wasn't much traffic on the main street at any time, but in the rain with the mud thickening, there was none. Virgil and I were silent.

"When we first got married," she said, "he was working in Saint Louis in a leather factory, cleaning hides. We was living in a room in a house near the factory. He used to smell terrible when he come home."

"Hides do stink," Virgil said.

"I was seventeen," she said. "I'd run off from home."

"And there you were," I said.

"And there I was," she said. "Only thing we had for decoration in the room was this old calendar that Bob hung on the wall. Wasn't even the right year. But it had a picture on it, of a little house in the middle of a field, with a tree over it, and a little stream running past. There was a man and woman standing outside the house with two little children beside them."

The Chinaman came out from the hotel kitchen with fresh coffee, and poured some in our cups. When he left,

Mrs. Redmond started talking again. I wasn't exactly sure how much she was talking to us.

"That's what we wanted, Bob maybe even more than me. And finally, when we got the homestead land out here, we thought we was going to have it."

"Nobody never really gets the pretty picture," I said.

"I guess not," she said. "Maybe if it wasn't for Wolfson . . ."

"There's always a Wolfson," Virgil said.

She nodded.

"He tried so hard," she said.

Her voice thickened as she spoke, and she sounded like she might cry.

"He's still trying. Trying to make a profit, trying to organize the other homesteaders to fight Wolfson . . ."

"And it ain't working out," I said.

"No," she said.

"And he's taking it out on you?" I said.

"I nagged him awful," she said.

Across the street, at the Excelsior, Cato and Rose came out on their porch and looked at the rain. Mrs. Redmond waved at them. Rose waved back.

"That Mr. Cato doesn't say much, does he," she said.

"Cato's his first name, ma'am," I said. "Cato Tillson. And no, he don't say much."

"He seems like a good man, though," she said.

I smiled.

"Depends on your definition," I said.

"Like how?" she said.

"Cato shoots people," Virgil said. "But he don't do it for the hell of it. And he ain't a back shooter. And he gives you his word, he keeps it."

"That's like you," Mrs. Redmond said.

"Some," Virgil said.

"Would he have really shot my husband that day in the saloon?" she said. "When he offered?"

"Oh, absolutely," I said.

The rain picked up a little so that it drummed hard on the shed roof of the porch, and the runoff formed almost a curtain between us and the street. We drank our coffee.

"I wish you could help him," Mrs. Redmond said after a time.

Neither Virgil nor I answered her. Across the street, Frank Rose was smoking a cigar, and the homey smell of it drifted through the rain to our porch.

"You still care about him," I said.

"Yes."

I nodded slowly.

"I know what you're thinking," she said. "You're thinking I'm with Virgil and . . ."

I nodded. She looked at Virgil. He didn't say anything.

"My husband was hurting me. I was alone, no money, no place to go. I was terrified. I couldn't see my children. Then Virgil come along and made all that go away. I am so grateful."

"Good reasons," I said.

She still looked at Virgil.

"Do you understand?" she said. "It ain't just all that. I care about you, but . . . do you understand?"

Virgil nodded slowly.

"I do," he said.

# 47.

It was a little after noon, with the sun out again, when a Cavalry lieutenant and a master sergeant showed up in front of the Blackfoot. They stopped their horses in front of where Virgil and I were taking in the sun. The lieutenant nodded at us, and the sergeant spoke.

"This town got a mayor?" he said.

"Nope," I said.

The sergeant looked at the lieutenant. The lieutenant took over.

"Town council?" he said.

"Nope."

"Sheriff?"

"Nope."

The lieutenant was annoyed.

"Marshal?"

I shook my head.

"So who the fuck is in charge around here?" the lieutenant said.

I thought about it for a minute.

"Well," I said, "fella named Wolfson owns the bank, the store, the hotel, the saloon, and the saloon across the street. I suppose he might be the one."

"Where do I find him?" the lieutenant said.

"Usually eats breakfast," I said, "'bout this time. In the saloon."

The lieutenant glanced up at the sun.

"Breakfast?" he said.

"Works late hours," I said.

The lieutenant nodded.

"Canavan," he said to the sergeant.

"Sir."

"See if you can find him and get him out here."

The sergeant swung down and went into the saloon. The lieutenant was quiet, looking around the town. Then he looked back at us.

"You work for this fella, Wolfson?" he said.

I nodded.

"You ain't bartenders," he said.

"No," I said.

"My name's Mulcahey," he said. "What's yours."

"Everett Hitch," I said. "This here's Virgil Cole."

Mulcahey looked at Virgil for a silent moment.

Then he said, "Heard of you."

Virgil nodded modestly.

"Any other gun hands in town?" Mulcahey said.

"Why do you ask?" Virgil said.

"Might need 'em," Mulcahey said.

"Couple of boys across the street," Virgil said, and nodded at the Excelsior. "Cato and Rose."

"They any good?" Mulcahey said.

He was talking to Virgil now instead of to me.

"Yes," Virgil said.

Sergeant Canavan came out of the Blackfoot with Wolfson.

"What can I do for you, Lieutenant," Wolfson said.

"You get things done in this town?" Mulcahey said.

"I like to think so," Wolfson said.

"A group of Shoshones jumped the reservation last night," Mulcahey said. "The rest of my platoon is rounding up the settlers south of town and herded them in here."

"Here? In town?"

"Yep, we need to make some arrangements to put them up until we get the Shoshones back where they belong," Mulcahey said. "How many can you put up here?"

"Here? In the hotel?"

"Hotel, livery stable, saloon, wherever we have to," Mulcahey said. "We leave them out there alone and the Shoshones can have them, one at a time."

"Who pays for this?" Wolfson said.

"Sergeant Canavan will give you a voucher," Mulcahey said. "We'll have them all in here by nightfall."

"You boys going to stick around?" Wolfson said.

"Nope, can't guard these people and chase the Shoshones," Mulcahey said.

"How many bucks," Virgil said.

"Maybe twenty," Mulcahey said.

"I didn't sign no contract," Wolfson said, "that I gotta protect every shitkicker that homesteads near me."

"I'm not asking you to do it," Mulcahey said. "I'm telling you you're going to."

# 48.

Wolfson assembled most of the men in the Blackfoot Saloon. Almost everybody had a weapon, mostly Winchesters, a few shotguns, and an occasional breech-loading Sharps.

"You all know why we're here," he said, "and why I volunteered to house and feed you all."

The women and children were housed in the hotel. The men were mostly sleeping on the floor in the Blackfoot and the Excelsior. In the hotel, the wives and the whores were a little uneasy with one another. And in the saloons the homesteader men were quite uneasy with those of us who worked for Wolfson. Beth and Bob Redmond moved around each other stiffly. And Stark and his lumberjacks were unhappy with everything. So was Wolfson. He'd had to hire another Chinaman to help in the kitchen cooking enough biscuits, beans, and salt meat for everybody. The Army vouchers would probably cover the cost, but there was unlikely to be any profit.

"The Army has asked me to take charge of the town defense until them red niggers is back where they belong," Wolfson said.

Virgil looked at me. I grinned and shrugged.

"Army says the bastards aren't in this area yet, but just to be sure," Wolfson said, "I got a couple lookouts up on the roof of the hotel right now ready to fire off a warning shot the minute they see anything."

Cato and Rose were drinking coffee at the bar near us. There were no liquor sales yet because of the meeting, but Frank Rose went behind the bar and got a bottle and poured a shot into his coffee, and left the bottle handy. Wolfson saw it and didn't like it but said nothing of it.

"First thing we got to do is to block off both ends of Main Street," Wolfson said. "Keep the buggers from getting in here and doing damage."

Cato and Rose both looked at Virgil. Virgil looked at me. I shook my head.

"'Scuse me, Amos," Virgil said.

Wolfson didn't like that, either, but he forced a smile.

"Y'all know Virgil Cole," Wolfson said, "one of the fellas works for me."

"Thing is, Amos," Virgil said, "if they was stupid enough

to come charging up the main street, I wouldn't want to discourage them. We could catch 'em in a crossfire and cut 'em in pieces."

"I don't want them in this town shooting up my property," Wolfson said.

"They ain't coming in the main street," Virgil said.

"They been fighting the Crows and the Arapaho for generations," I said. "They know how to fight. They ain't going to ride into a shooting gallery."

"So you're saying don't block the street."

Virgil nodded.

"Everett's right," he said. "They ain't going to ride in and let us catch them in a crossfire, but there's no reason to make it difficult, case they want to."

Redmond was standing in front of Wolfson.

"So what are we supposed to do?" Redmond said.

"Everett here is a graduate of the United States Military Academy at West Point, New York," Virgil said. "He's done some Indian fighting in his time."

He made a gesture with his head that said, *You tell them.*

"Lookouts on the roof are good," I said, to make Wolfson feel good. "And we need to organize our manpower, break down into squads, for instance, so that we can mobilize quickly if we have to."

I looked at Fritz Stark.

"You take care of that with your people?"

"We're already in crews," Stark said.

"Good," I said. "Redmond, you want to organize yours?"

"How many people in a squad?" Redmond said.

"Depends how many people you got," I said. "I'll help you."

Redmond nodded.

"We're ready to do what has to be done," he said.

Virgil smiled slightly.

Frank Rose murmured, "Hooray!"

"Wolfson can manage the miners and the town folks," I said. "And we'll need some pickets."

"Outside the town?" Redmond said.

"Wouldn't be much use inside the town, now would they," Wolfson said.

"That'll be us," Virgil said.

"Us?" Redmond said.

"Me and Everett," Virgil said. "Cato and Rose."

Everybody in the room, that I could see, looked relieved.

# 49.

It was a bright night. Lot of stars. Moon nearly full.
Virgil and I were riding as soft as we could along the
tree line uphill from the town.

"Think they'll do what we told 'em?" I said. "If the Shoshones actually make a run at them?"

"Probably not," Virgil said.

"On the other hand, the Shoshones probably won't make a
run at them. There's what, twenty of them, Mulcahey said?"

"Yep."

A night bird whistled in the woods. Both of us reined in
and sat silently. The bird whistled again.

"Bird," I said.

"Yep," Virgil said.

We started the horses again.

"And maybe a hundred men with guns in the town?"

"At least," Virgil said.

"So the Shoshones aren't going to make a run at them."

"Probably not," Virgil said.

"They might come by the homesteads," I said, "thinking they might pick off a homesteader or two, burn a couple ranches, run off some stock."

"That's right," Virgil said. "Same for the lumber company."

"So we come across them doing this," I said, "we do anything?"

"We got four fighters," Virgil said.

"We got a hundred men," I said.

"And four fighters," Virgil said.

I nodded.

"So we head back to town and keep the people safe," I said.

"Uh-huh."

"Hard for a lot of them to come back," I said, "they get burned out."

"Harder to come back from getting killed," Virgil said.

"And it's worth remembering that unless the Shoshones split up, there's twenty of them and two of us, at any given time."

"Shoshones won't split up," Virgil said.

"No," I said.

"And if they get past us and into the town and we're not there, and Cato and Rose aren't there, it'll be a bloodbath."

"You don't think Wolfson can rally the troops?"

"Redmond, either," Virgil said. "Stark maybe, but . . . he's not a gunman."

"And Wolfson and Redmond would be fighting so hard to be in charge that they'd get in his way even if he was," I said.

Virgil held his horse suddenly. I stopped with him. Virgil listened hard. I hadn't heard anything, and I still didn't. After a little bit, Virgil nodded to himself and moved his horse forward again. I went with him.

"Hear something?" I said.

"Nothing that matters," Virgil said.

We rode on.

"How are things going with you and Mrs. Redmond?" I said.

"Her children are with her," Virgil said.

"And her husband's downstairs," I said.

"That's right."

"So things ain't going at all," I said.

"That's right."

"Sorry to hear that," I said.

"Things change," Virgil said.

"Ever think about Allie?" I said.

"Yes."

I couldn't think of anything to say about that, so I moved to a different subject.

"Funny thing about Wolfson and Redmond," I said. "First I thought they just wanted to get ahead in their own way."

"Probably do," Virgil said.

"Redmond's stuck," I said. "But Wolfson ain't. He got ahead. He runs the damn town, and he still ain't happy."

"He don't run the town," Virgil said.

"Who does?"

"We do," Virgil said.

# 50.

The Shoshones came in, south of town, about twelve hours ahead of the Army and set fire to the settlements. The smoke hovered over the town, and one of the lookouts fired off a warning shot, claiming Indians were upon us. Everyone with a weapon grabbed it and rushed to find a place to shoot from.

"They ain't much of a threat to the Shoshones," Frank Rose said. "But they're likely to inflict considerable casualties on each other."

"Guess we better take a look," Virgil said.

"If the farmers don't shoot at us," Rose said.

"If they do, they'll probably miss," I said.

There was no sign of anyone in the area where the lookout had seen the hostiles. On horseback we slowly began to circle the town. The smoke from the burning settlements was plain enough, and the smell of it was strong. At the top of a small rise between the town and the settlements we saw two bucks. One had what looked like an old Army-issue Sharps. The other wore a Cavalry campaign hat and carried a button-flap holster that had probably been taken from a soldier someplace. We stopped. The Indians stopped. We looked at one another.

"There's more of us than them," Rose said.

"That we can see," Virgil said.

"True," Rose said.

"Don't want to go charging after them and run right into eighteen more of them behind the rise," I said.

We continued to sit with the smoke billowing up behind the Indians, and the pleasant breeze blowing it toward us. The Indians rode back and forth in front of us. The one with the Sharps brandished it at us. The guy with the campaign hat waved it at us.

"They think they're out of our range," Virgil said.

"They ain't," Cato said.

"You want to do it?" Virgil said.

"Sure."

Cato handed the reins to Rose and slid off his horse. He took his rifle from the saddle and stepped away from his horse. He cocked the hammer, raised the rifle, let his breath out softly, and squeezed the trigger. The Indian with the Sharps slumped and then fell from his saddle. The other Indian gazed at him for a minute and then spun his horse. The gaze cost him. Cato hit him in the back between the shoulder blades as the Indian kicked his horse into a run. The Indian tossed forward over the horse's neck and onto the ground. The two horses trotted a few feet and stopped and looked at the dead Indians, and began to crop the grass. Cato put two fresh rounds in his rifle, slid it back in the scabbard, and remounted.

We sat some more. No Indians came boiling over the rise. The horses continued to graze. The smoke continued overhead darkly. Virgil nudged his horse forward, and the rest of us followed. We rode slowly up to the two Indians. Both were dead. Neither was very old.

There was no sign of anyone downslope. Virgil dismounted and walked to the two horses. They looked at him. He took the primitive rope bridles off both horses. The horses went back to eating. Virgil left the rope on the ground and got back on his horse.

"Two kids," he said, "showin' off."

"Whoever," Rose said. "We just improved the odds a little."

"We did," Virgil said. And we turned our horses back to town.

# 51.

Two days later, Sergeant Canavan came into the Blackfoot, which was still bristling with guns. He smiled
faintly when he saw them.

Then he came to Virgil and me and said, "Where's that
fella in charge?"

"Wolfson?" I said.

"Yeah," Canavan said, "him."

"Don't know," I said. "You can talk to us."

"Bet I can," Canavan said.

He looked around at the armed settlers everywhere.
Again, he smiled faintly.

"Lieutenant Mulcahey wants you to know that we got the
hostiles. Killed three, herded the rest of them back onto the
reservation."

"So we can call off the siege," I said.

Canavan grinned.

"You can call off the siege," he said. "Found a couple of 'em dead, south of town. That your doing?"

"Wasn't very old," Virgil said.

"Old enough," Canavan said. "One of 'em had a trooper's gun and hat."

"Anything left out there?" I said. "For these people to go back to?"

"Nope."

"Settlements?" I said.

"Burned all the buildings, killed any stock they could find."

"Copper mine?"

"Burned pretty much everything that would burn," Canavan said. "Missed the lumber camp for some reason."

"Too bad you didn't get them sooner," I said.

"They slaughtered five people, west of here," Canavan said.

"Okay," I said. "Coulda been worse."

"You'll tell whatsisname Wolfson?" he said.

"We will," I said.

"Thanks," Canavan said.

"Want a drink 'fore you go?" Virgil said.

"No, thanks, got too far to go, and got to ride too hard," Canavan said. "Have one for me."

He looked around at the armed settlers.

"Don't let them open fire till I'm out of range," he said.

"War's over," I yelled. "Don't shoot the soldier."

Most of the men in the room heard me. They stared at

me, as Canavan with a big grin walked out of the saloon door and swung back up on his horse.

"What's that about the war?" Redmond said.

"Indians are back on the reservation," I said. "You can put the weapons away."

"Sergeant tell you that?" Redmond said.

"He did," I said.

Redmond turned to the crowd.

"We've defeated the savages," Redmond shouted.

He stepped up onto a chair.

"It's over," he shouted. "We've won."

Wolfson came in from the hotel.

"What's that?" he said.

"Indians are back on the reservation," Virgil said to him.

"By God," Wolfson said. "By God."

He looked around at the men and at Redmond standing on a chair in front of them.

"Drinks are on me," he shouted.

"No," Virgil said.

"What?"

"Not until they put the guns away," Virgil said.

Wolfson stared for a moment. Cato and Rose and I blocked access to the bar.

"I don't like being told what to do by one of my fucking employees," Wolfson said.

"You want a room full of armed drunks?" Virgil said.

Wolfson looked slightly startled. Then he shook his head and walked to the back of the saloon, and opened a store-room door.

"Stash your weapons here," he shouted, "then drink up."

Virgil stood by the door as people put Winchesters and shotguns and an occasional sidearm into the storeroom. When everyone had done it, Virgil nodded at me, and the three of us stepped away from the bar. Virgil put a chair in front of the storeroom door and sat in it. I walked over and joined him.

Frank Rose said to Wolfson, "This gonna happen across the street?"

"Absolutely," Wolfson said. "I'm heading over there now to let them know."

"Same rules apply," Rose said. "No guns."

"This is my town, and we got plenty to celebrate."

"No guns," Rose said.

Wolfson shrugged. Rose nodded and looked at Cato, and the two of them walked out of the Blackfoot. Wolfson hurried behind them.

"Let me make the announcement," he said. "Let me make the announcement."

"You can do anything you want, Amos," Rose said, "long as there's no guns. Me and Cato hate drunks with guns."

# 52.

Wolfson was having a meeting at a table in the Blackfoot. Hensdale was there, and Stark. Faison was at the table, and so was Bob Redmond. Virgil and I sat nearby and drank coffee with Cato and Rose, and listened.

"I can't keep housing all these fucking people," Wolfson said.

"My miners are ready to move on," Faison said. "Mine's pretty well run out anyway. You pay us the two weeks' wages you owe us and we'll find another mine."

"Two weeks' wages?" Wolfson said. "I been housing you for nothing."

"You been letting us sleep on the floor of your fucking saloon," Faison said. "Ain't the same."

"I gotta think 'bout them two weeks' wages," Wolfson said. "I don't know what you did to earn it."

"You think about it all you want," Faison said. "But I go back and tell my miners you ain't paying, you gonna have a visit from all of us."

"Hear that, Virgil," Wolfson said. "Sounds like a threat to me."

"That's what it sounds like," Virgil said.

"Everything's gone," Faison said. "Bunkhouses, cook shack, mine office, and there ain't enough copper left in that mine to pay for breakfast."

"Ain't my fault," Wolfson said.

"Ain't ours, either," Faison said. "Mine ain't worth saving. We know that. But you got to pay us so we can move on."

"I ain't made a penny," Wolfson said, "since the fucking Indians left the reservation. I got you and these fucking homesteaders sprawled all over my property, eating my food. Who pays for that? Who pays for the fucking lumberjacks been eating everything but the fucking bar?"

"I'll cover my people," Stark said.

"Yeah? Who covers the shitkickers? They got no money," Wolfson said. "They got no way to earn any. They owe me already, and all the collateral I got is their property, which is now mostly fucking cinders."

"We're not quitters," Redmond said. "We can start over."

"Start over?" Wolfson said. "Start over with what? I put myself in the fucking poorhouse giving you cocksuckers credit, and what do I get? A chance to fucking feed you and house you at my cost."

"For Jesus' sake, Wolfson," Redmond said. "We got no place to go."

"Well, find someplace, because I'm through."

"There's women," Redmond said. I thought he might have glanced quickly at Virgil. "And kids."

"Fuck 'em," Wolfson said. "Women, kids, everybody. All you got to give me is your land, and that ain't worth much."

"Land?"

"I'm taking the land," Wolfson said. "You people owe me ten times what it's worth, but it's all there is."

"You can't just take our land," Redmond said.

"Can," Wolfson said. "Will. So you and your women and children and sodbusters and shitkickers and chicken wranglers get the fuck out of my town."

"We're not going," Redmond said. "We got no place to go."

"You'll go or I'll run you out," Wolfson said.

Redmond looked at us.

"You'd do that?" he said to us. "If he told you to, you'd run off a bunch of hard-working homesteaders, kids and everything?"

None of us said anything.

"Money talks," Wolfson said. "You're the only one doesn't get that, Redmond."

"You folks can come up to the lumber camp," Stark said.

Everyone looked at him.

"It's rough, but we'll make do till you get back on your feet."

"They ain't gonna get back on their feet, Fritzie," Wolfson said. "Don't you get it? They got nothing."

Stark stared at Wolfson for a time.

Then he said, "Wolfson, you are a fucking scavenger. You got no more heart than a fucking buzzard."

"Fritzie," Wolfson said.

"Don't call me Fritzie, you walleyed cocksucker," Stark said. "I don't care how many gunmen you hire. Redmond, you bring your people up to my place today. We'll work something out."

"Mind if I sit in on that?" Faison said.

"You're welcome to," Stark said.

Then Stark got to his feet and turned his back to Wolfson and walked out of the saloon. Redmond and Faison got up and followed.

I looked at Virgil. He looked back at me and grinned.

"What'd I tell you about Stark?" he said.

# 53.

The settlers moved up to the lumber camp, and the miners joined them. Wolfson was away. Resolution was nearly empty. There was no money being spent, because nobody had any. The saloons were deathly silent, and with nothing better to do, Virgil and I rode out and looked at the burned-out homesteads.

The Shoshones had been effective. There wasn't much to see: the barely recognizable remnant of a dead farm animal, a chimney that hadn't burned, some scraps of harness, the metal prongs of a rake. A solitary buzzard circled in the sky, without much enthusiasm. Everything edible had been scavenged already. But with regularity along the trail through the settlements there were signs that said the same thing: NO TRESPASSING, *per order Amos Wolfson, Owner.*

"Think it's legal," Virgil said, "Wolfson taking their land?"

"Might be," I said. "Don't really know. I think it's homestead land."

"That make a difference?" Virgil said.

"I'd think so, but I don't know."

"Didn't teach you 'bout real-estate law at West Point?" Virgil said.

"Nope. Know a lot about the Macedonian phalanx, though."

"What the fuck is that?" Virgil said.

I explained.

"They taught you that at West Point?" Virgil said.

"Yep."

"We ain't been fighting with pikes for a while," Virgil said.

"War department hadn't caught on to that when I was there," I said.

We moved on through the homesteads. Near the buildings, fresh new shoots of green were already beginning to push up through the burnt-over grass. At the top of the rise where we'd left them were the remains of the two Shoshone warriors we'd killed. There wasn't much left of them. Their horses had long since drifted off, probably homing back to the reservation, the way horses do. Buzzards, coyotes, maybe a wolf, maybe a bear, maybe a cougar, certainly insects and other birds, had fed on them until there was nothing much to feed on. Their weapons were still with them. Something had even eaten at the holster that one of them had worn.

The pistol was starting to rust. So was the old rifle. We sat our horses for a time, looking at the remains.

"Don't seem right," Virgil said. "He can just take everything they got."

"No," I said. "It don't."

"Don't seem like it would be legal," Virgil said.

"Don't matter none," I said. "Legal, illegal. There's not any law around here anyway."

"'Cept us," Virgil said.

"What do we do when Wolfson tells us to move them off the land?" I said.

"Been thinking on that," Virgil said.

He kept looking at the skeletal remnants of the two Indians.

"Can't keep taking a man's money," Virgil said finally, "and keep saying no to what he wants you to do."

"I know," I said.

"Can't run them people off their land," Virgil said.

"I know," I said.

# 54.

Virgil and I were on the front porch of the Blackfoot, admiring the early evening, when Beth Redmond came down the street with her skirts tucked up, astride one of those nondescript, big-boned horses that a lot of sodbusters had, because they could afford only one. When she reached us she held her skirts down and swung her left leg over the horse and slid modestly off him on the side away from us. Then she came around, hitched the horse, and came up on the porch and sat on the railing opposite us with her feet dangling.

"Evenin', Beth," Virgil said.

"Hello," she said. "Hello, Mr. Hitch."

I nodded toward her.

"Mrs. Redmond."

"Virgil, we have to talk," she said.

"Talk in front of Everett," Virgil said. "I'd just tell him later anyway."

"He knows about us?" she said.

"Yep."

"That's a little embarrassing," she said.

"Everett don't care," Virgil said.

"But I might," she said.

"Suppose you might," Virgil said. "Hadn't thought of that."

I stood.

"I can go," I said.

She shook her head rapidly.

"No," she said. "Stay. What I'm talking about will include you, too."

I sat.

"We ain't going to leave," she said.

"You and Redmond?" Virgil said.

"None of us," she said. "Mr. Stark's going to help us rebuild. He'll give us the lumber on credit. He'll give some of the men jobs in the lumber camp."

"Wolfson already put up signs on the land," I said. "He says it's his now."

"We won't let him take it," Mrs. Redmond said.

Neither Virgil nor I said anything.

"Since the Indians," she said, "when we were all together, and armed, and ready. The men feel like they won, and can win again."

"Mrs. Redmond," I said. "They didn't see an Indian."

"Please call me Beth," she said. "I know. But they were ready, and it makes them feel better. And Mr. Stark is making them feel better. They ain't felt good for an awful long time. They need to do this."

I nodded. Virgil nodded.

"Stark gonna help you when the guns come?" Virgil said.

"He said he would."

"Bunch of lumberjacks," Virgil said.

"They're tough men," she said.

"With a peavey," Virgil said. "Guns are a little different."

"I know," Beth said. "But we ain't gonna go."

"How 'bout you and your husband," Virgil said.

"It's the same thing as the rest," Beth said. "When we was all here, and the Indians was coming, and everybody had a gun, he felt like he was protecting me and the kids. He felt like he was the leader of his friends. He felt good."

"He know 'bout us?" Virgil said.

"Yes."

"How's he feel 'bout that?" Virgil said.

"He thinks he deserved it," Beth said. "For beating me up and everything. Swears that he's a changed man now. Swears that he'll never hit me again."

I knew Virgil would not ask, so I did.

"You and him back together, then?" I said.

"Yes."

She looked sideways at Virgil. Virgil nodded.

"I'm sorry, Virgil," she said. "You've been a good friend."

"Perfectly fine," Virgil said.

No one spoke. The nondescript plow horse was scratching the underside of his jaw on the hitching rail. We all watched him.

Then Virgil said, "You got something else, Beth."

She nodded.

"I . . ." She stopped and then tried again. "I . . ."

She stopped and looked wordlessly at Virgil.

"You want us to help you," Virgil said.

"Help him," she said. "Help the men. Don't run them off, no matter what Wolfson says."

Virgil nodded.

"Can you do that for me?" Beth said.

Virgil didn't speak for a while. I waited. Beth waited.

Then he said, "I won't run them off."

Beth looked at me.

"Mr. Hitch?"

"Everett," I said.

"Will you run them off, Everett?" she said.

"No," I said. "I'm with Virgil."

"What about the other two," she said.

Now that it was out, she was emptying the pitcher.

"I'll talk to them," Virgil said.

"Will they listen to you?"

"Yes," Virgil said.

"And Mr. Wolfson, what will he do?" she said.

"Hire other people," Virgil said.

"And what will you do then?" Beth said.

It was out, and we were all looking at it. None of us said anything for a time.

Finally, Virgil said, "Step at a time, Beth. Step at a time."

# 55.

Wolfson got ahead of us. He came back from his travels with a big-bodied, dark-haired man named Major Lujack.

"Major Lujack is the head of Lujack Detective Agency in Wichita," Wolfson said. "And a retired Cavalry officer."

"Battle of Muddy River?" I said.

Lujack looked at me and nodded.

"You've heard of Major Lujack?" Wolfson said.

"Slaughtered a camp full of Comanche women and children," I said. "In eastern Colorado. While back. Got a medal for it, and was discharged two weeks later."

"Everett's retired Army, too," Virgil said.

"It was an honorable discharge," Lujack said.

"Army covered it up," I said. "Made it sound like a battle. But they got rid of you."

"Who's this?" Virgil said.

He was looking at a willowy, round-faced, sloe-eyed man with a flat crowned hat and striped pants, who was standing next to Lujack.

"My assistant," Lujack said. "Mr. Swann."

"I'm Mr. Cole," Virgil said. "This is Mr. Hitch."

Swann nodded.

"Major Lujack is here to help us with the settlers and all," Wolfson said. "The rest of his people will be arriving soon."

Both Lujack and Swann wore guns. They seemed comfortable with them.

"How many," Virgil said.

"Three squads of five men and a squad leader," Lujack said.

"Plus you and Mr. Swann," Virgil said. "So twenty."

"Yes," Lujack said.

Virgil was looking at Swann. Swann was looking back at Virgil.

"You fellas have had a long ride," Wolfson said. "Lemme show you your rooms."

"Certainly," Lujack said.

He looked at me. Swann looked hard at Virgil. Then they turned and followed Wolfson.

"Whaddya know about Lujack?" Virgil said.

"He's a butcher," I said.

"Why'd he do it?"

"Don't know," I said. "Don't know why he even attacked them. There wasn't a warrior within fifty miles."

"And the Army gave him the boot?"

"Yeah. Some of his command had refused to keep up the killing once they realized they weren't fighting men. Afterwards, he was in the process of court-martialing them."

"Insubordination?" Virgil said.

I grinned.

"Desertion," I said. "In the face of the enemy."

"Even the Army couldn't stomach it," Virgil said.

"That's right," I said. "They called it a victory, promoted him to major, cancelled the court-martial process, and gave him an honorable discharge."

"Three squads," Virgil said. "Each with a squad leader."

"Plus Lujack and Swann," I said. "You know anything 'bout Mr. Swann."

"Pretty much all I need to," Virgil said.

"Ever hear of him?" I said.

"Nope," Virgil said.

"But you know what he is," I said.

"I do," Virgil said. "You?"

"Yeah," I said. "I know what he is."

"Might be we're being replaced," Virgil said.

"Do look kind of suspicious," I said. "How 'bout Cato and Rose."

"Days are numbered," Virgil said. "But Wolfson'll wait until all the squads arrive. Case we resent it."

"We gonna resent it?" I said.

"Hell, no," Virgil said. "Makes it easier to change sides."

# 56.

The squads drifted into town over the next few days, set up tents, and dug latrines out back of the hotel. A lot of them appeared to be ex-soldiers. No one was in uniform. But there was a military tone to things, and everyone wore badges that said *Lujack Detective*.

"Heard about Lujack," Frank Rose was saying. "Offered me a job once."

"Think he remembers?" I said.

"Hell no," Rose said. "I never talked with him. His bitch buddy does most of the early hiring work."

"Swann?"

"Yep. And Lujack makes the final call."

"And you didn't get that far?" I said.

"Did," Rose said. "But I didn't like Swann. So I never showed up for Lujack."

"How's he work?" Virgil said.

"Pretends he's still a major," Rose said. "Runs things like a military unit. Chain of command, all that shit."

"Ah, yes," I said. "One of the many reasons I left."

"Got a lot of bad, mean people working for him," Rose said. "And he keeps them in line."

"They good?" Virgil said.

"Yeah," Rose said. "Lujack don't hire no virgins. They know what they're doing and they're willin' to do it."

"Puts them ahead of the collection of gasbags," I said, "that Wolfson brought in before."

"The way it works," Rose said, "you hire Lujack. Lujack hires everybody else."

"And pays them," Virgil said.

"Yep. You pay Lujack," Rose said. "Lujack pays them."

"So their loyalty is always to Lujack," I said.

"Yep."

"Look at the Winchesters," I said.

"What about them."

There were three pyramid-shaped clusters of rifles.

"They've stacked arms for each squad," I said.

"One stack per squad," Rose said.

We all looked at the rifles. We all smiled.

"See that fella there," Cato said, "with the big yella mustache? And the black handle Colt? Saw him kill three men in Ellsworth. They had words in the street."

Cato gestured as if shooting.

"Bang, bang, bang," he said. "One bullet each."

And made a falling gesture with both hands.

"Hope the words mattered," Rose said.

"Don't matter much anymore," Cato said.

It might have been the most I'd heard him talk since he'd arrived.

"Figure they'll get through setting up today?" I said.

"Sure," Rose said. "Hell, they're almost there now."

"So you think Wolfson'll fire us tonight?" I said.

Rose shrugged.

"If he brings them all in for a meetin'," Virgil said. "You'll know."

# 57.

Wolfson had his meeting. He sat at a back table in the Blackfoot, with Swann on one side of him and Lujack on the other. The three squads stood against the wall on either side of the room.

"Boys," Wolfson said to the four of us standing in front of the table. "We're gonna have to make a change."

None of us spoke.

"You boys done a fine job keepin' the peace here in Resolution," Wolfson said. "But we all knew it was only temporary, and, well, now we got what you might call permanent cadre here, and there just ain't no need for you fellas."

"Don't fuck with it, Wolfson," Virgil said. "Just fire us."

"Well, I wouldn't want you to think of it as getting fired,"

Wolfson said. "I like you boys. It's just that you, ah, served your term, you know?"

Cato Tillson looked slowly around the room, snorted silently to himself, and walked out. Wolfson watched him and didn't say anything for a moment. Then he refocused on the rest of us.

"I've asked Major Lujack to be town marshal," Wolfson said.

"With nineteen deputies," Rose said.

"Exactly."

"I figure you owe me four days' pay," Rose said.

"I do," Wolfson said. "And I'm happy to give all of you what I owe you. And room and board through the end of the week . . . plus a nice bonus for the job you did."

"When do I get the money?" Rose said.

"Tomorrow. See Hensdale anytime tomorrow," Wolfson said. "All of you."

"I will," Rose said, and headed for the door.

Wolfson looked at Virgil and me.

"You boys been with me the longest," Wolfson said. "And I want to thank you both special."

"Amos," I said, "I'm too old to listen to horseshit. I'll stop by and see Hensdale."

"Well, just so there's no hard feelings," Wolfson said.

"None," I said.

"You, Virgil?" Wolfson said.

"No feelings at all," Virgil said.

Wolfson nodded. There didn't seem to be anything else to say. But nobody ended it, and Virgil, for whatever reason,

didn't seem quite through yet. I didn't know what his reason was, but Virgil was never a creature of whim, he was
doing something. What he appeared to be doing was looking at Swann. Swann looked back.

Finally, Lujack said, "'Fore you boys go, I'd be interested
in your plans."

"Got no plans," I said.

Virgil continued looking at Swann, as if Swann was an
odd specimen of something.

"You, Cole?" Lujack said.

"None," Virgil said.

Then I realized what Virgil was doing. He was pretty sure
he'd have to go against Swann one day, and he was getting
to know him as well as he could in preparation for that.

"Well," Lujack said. "That'll be fine for a few days, while
you get your affairs in order. But in a week or so, I'll be asking you all to move on."

"We'll keep it in mind," I said.

Swann continued to meet Virgil's stare. But it was a waste
of his time. Virgil was probably unlike anyone Swann had
ever seen. Virgil didn't care if you met his stare or not. He
didn't care if he intimidated you or not. He was just gather-
ing information.

"You got any plans, Cole?" Lujack said.

Without taking his eyes off Swann, Virgil said, "I'm formulatin'."

"And you heard me," Lujack said, "about not hanging
around too long."

"I did," Virgil said.

"Hope you'll keep it in mind," Lujack said.

"Surely will," Virgil said.

He continued to look at Swann.

"Would," Swann said to Virgil, "I was you."

"One of the things I'm real happy about," Virgil said, "is you ain't me."

They looked at each other for another minute. Then Virgil nodded to himself as if he'd learned something and turned and walked out. I went with him.

# 58.

Virgil and I were sitting out front of the Excelsior, formulatin' with Cato and Rose, when the new marshal and his deputies rode out of town in a neat column of twos, heading south. Virgil stood as they went by.

"Think I'll go along behind them," he said, "for observatory purposes."

"Might as well go along," I said. "Being as how I got no job."

"None of us got a job," Rose said. "Me and Cato may as well tag along."

Twenty horses, riding in a column on a dry dirt road, kicked up enough dust so we had no trouble keeping track. We rode together at an easy pace far enough behind them so's not to cause a stir.

The trail ran out through the settlements in a series of small, low hills that stepped down to the level ground. As we came to the top of one of them, we could see a homestead below us. There was a lumber wagon, and several men were unloading lumber beside a half-built house frame. Lujack and his men rode on down to the property. The four of us stopped on the top of the small rise and watched.

The two columns peeled left and right as they reached the property. Nine men in either direction, with Lujack and Swann in the center. The horsemen stopped and sat their mounts. Lujack spoke to the men building the house, and one of them stopped work and came forward. He talked with Lujack. As the conversation proceeded, the man got more and more excited, waving his arms, pointing at the half-built house. Finally, the man stopped speaking and folded his arms and stood. Lujack said something to Swann.

With a fluid motion, Swann drew his gun and shot the man. The sound of the shot rolled past us at the top of the hill. You could tell the man was dead by the way he went down. And afterward, the clenched void of silence.

Below us, everyone seemed painted on a backdrop until Lujack spoke to the workmen. They listened. Then Lujack made a hand gesture and the company wheeled and he led them out, once again in a column of twos, raising dust as they came back up the rise, and past us, where we sat on our horses.

No one said anything, and the column passed with no sound but the horses' hooves on the dusty trail, and the jingle of spurs and bridle trim. Neither Lujack nor Swann paid us any attention.

As the column disappeared over the next rise, the men below gathered around the man whom Swann had shot. After a time they put him in the bed of the near-empty lumber wagon and laid him out as best they could. Then the teamster and another man climbed up and turned the wagon, and the horses plodded up the hill, kicking up some dust of their own, as they trailed the marshal and his deputies back into town.

"Major Lujack don't appear to take criticism well," Rose said.

"You want to pull out of here?" I said to Virgil. "And go find Allie?"

"Not yet," Virgil said.

"You boys got anyplace to go?" I said to Cato and Rose.

"Nope," Rose said.

"There's twenty of them," I said, "and four of us."

"Not if we pick off a few," Cato said.

Virgil looked down at the half-built house. The rest of the workers had scattered, and nothing moved. He turned his horse then, and rode slowly after the wagon. The rest of us followed.

"We'll think on it," he said.

# 59.

Virgil decided that it was time to try out the old sorrel mare, see if her gashed leg had healed and she was sound. I went with him because I had nowhere else to go, and we rode easily up the hill north of town and sat the horses in the shade just inside the tree line.

Virgil got off the mare and picked up her foreleg. He looked at it and squeezed it gently and put it down and remounted. The mare cropped a little grass. Virgil patted her neck.

"Good as new," he said.

"Which ain't all that good," I said.

"Nope," Virgil said, "she ain't much. But what there is of her is working fine."

We looked down at the town below us. It wasn't much, either. They were building a town marshal's office next to the Blackfoot, on the north side. While we watched, a squad of new deputy marshals rode down Main Street and south out of town.

"You remember," Virgil said as we watched them ride out, "how we got to be the law in Appaloosa?"

"Them three fellas, owned businesses in town, they hired us," I said.

"Town council."

"So they said."

"Anybody elect them?" Virgil asked.

"Not that I know of," I said.

The squad of deputies disappeared over the crest of the first hill south of town and reappeared at the crest of the next one.

"We had a set of laws," Virgil said, "written out clear."

"And we wrote them," I said.

Virgil nodded.

"So this collection of vermin," he said, "is as much the law here as we was in Appaloosa."

"I guess so," I said.

The squad went over the next hill, where the road curved, following the creek.

"We done the right thing," Virgil said, "best we could, in Appaloosa."

"Yep."

The deputies were out of sight now.

"These people won't do the right thing," Virgil said.

"Not likely," I said.

"Already done the wrong thing, shooting that sodbuster," Virgil said.

"I'd say so."

"And they're the law."

"'Fraid so," I said.

Virgil nodded his head slowly, gazing downhill at the ugly little town.

"Not much of a place," he said.

"No," I said.

"Getting worse," Virgil said. "Mine's dried up. Lumber company's out of business, at least for now. Homesteaders been run off the land."

"Yep."

"There's no money to be spent," Virgil said. "Nobody to borrow from the bank. Nobody to buy feed at the emporium. No beef to broker. Whiskey sales are almost nothing in the saloons."

"Hard to make a profit," I said, "by eliminatin' your customers."

"Whole fucking town is going under," Virgil said.

"Seems so," I said.

"And Wolfson wants it," Virgil said.

"Yep."

"Why?" Virgil said.

"He probably don't know, either," I said.

"Don't seem worth killing folks over."

"Hell, Virgil," I said. "You know better'n I do that people kill folks for nothing at all."

Virgil nodded again.

"They do," he said.

Then he clucked to the mare and we rode on back down the hill.

# 60.

We were sitting with Cato and Rose at a table in the Excelsior, where they no longer worked. They didn't act like they didn't work there. When Virgil and I came in, Rose went behind the bar and got four glasses and a bottle and brought them out.

"Nice thing," Rose said, "'bout being out of work, gives you time to sit around and drink whiskey."

We all sipped the first sip. I could feel it seep happily through me.

"Whaddya do when you're working, Frank?" Virgil said.

Rose looked at him. He was puzzled.

"Same as you," he said.

"And what's that?" Virgil said.

Rose looked at him some more.

"Shootin'," he said, and grinned, "or threatenin' to."

"That bother you?"

Rose looked surprised.

"Shootin' people?" he said. "No."

"You, Cato?"

Cato shook his head.

"Everett?"

"Depends on who I'm shootin'," I said.

"And why," Cato said.

All three of us looked at him. It was always surprising when Cato spoke.

"Right," Rose said. "I mean, I ain't gonna back-shoot nobody, or shoot no women or kids."

"How 'bout that sodbuster got killed the other day?" Virgil said.

"No," Rose said. "That was wrong. Me and Cato both think that was wrong."

Cato nodded.

"You was working for Wolfson still, would you do it?" Virgil said.

Rose thought about it for a minute. He looked at Cato. Then he said, "No, neither one of us."

Cato nodded briefly.

"Everett?" Virgil said.

I shook my head.

"Probably not."

Virgil nodded.

We all drank a little more.

"What's bothering you, Virgil?" Rose said. "You know what we are, what we do. What the hell are all these questions?"

Virgil shook his head and sipped another taste of whiskey.

"So you shoot who you want and not who you don't want," Virgil said.

"Yeah," Rose said.

Cato nodded.

"Because you can," he said.

"Pretty much," Rose said.

He looked at me.

"You, Everett?"

"Yeah," I said.

Virgil stared into his whiskey for a moment, then drank some.

"You think Swann feels that way?" he said.

"Naw," Rose said.

"So how's he decide?" Virgil said.

"He don't," Rose said. "He'll shoot anybody he can get away with."

"He likes it," Cato said.

"And we don't?" Virgil said.

Rose shrugged.

"Me and Cato don't. I mean, we don't mind. But it's not a thrill or nothing."

"So why do it?" Virgil said.

"Because we're good at it, and it ain't hard work," Rose said. "'Cept if you get killed."

Cato nodded.

"People always gonna kill other people," Rose said. "Always gonna be fellas like us, that are good at it. And there'll be fellas like Swann who are good at it, too."

"So if you're good with a gun," Virgil said, "you can shoot people or not."

"Uh-huh," Rose said.

"And who decides?"

"Me," Rose said.

Cato and I both nodded. Virgil stared further at his whiskey.

"Don't seem the way it oughta be," Virgil said.

"Don't," I said.

"But it is," Virgil said.

"Ain't much else," I said.

# 61.

Some men behind a stone outcropping drew down on us with Winchesters as Virgil and I rode up to the lumber camp.

"Name's Virgil Cole," Virgil said. "Tell Stark me 'n Hitch come to talk with him and Redmond."

There was some scurrying around through the woods while we sat our horses, and after a time we got to go ride in. It was an odd-looking lumber camp. Tents pitched. Cook fires going. Children scrambling around. Women doing laundry. Stark and Redmond were on the steps of the lumber shack.

"'Fore you get off them horses," Stark said, "I want to know why you're here."

"We was thinking we might give you a hand," Virgil said.

"With what?"

"Wolfson."

Stark looked at us for a moment.

"You and Hitch?" he said to Virgil.

"Me 'n Everett," Virgil said. "Cato and Rose."

Stark and Redmond were silent for a moment.

Then Stark said, "You four?"

"Yep."

"Why?" Redmond said.

He was looking hard at Virgil.

"Seems like a good idea," Virgil said.

"That's all?" Redmond said.

"Either we climb down and talk about this," Virgil said, "or we turn around and ride back out. "

"Climb down," Stark said. "We'll sit outside. It's a little close inside."

We sat on the front steps of the lumber shack.

"Lujack and Swann and their people rode out and killed one of your people," Virgil said.

"Ty Harrison," Redmond said. "A fine man."

"Sure," Virgil said. "You folks gonna stick it out?"

"We ain't running," Redmond said.

"Next sodbuster starts to rebuild, same thing's going to happen," I said.

"Next time, we'll go in force," Redmond said.

Virgil ignored him. He looked at Stark.

"What do you say, Stark?"

"Lujack and his people," Stark said. "They're good."

"Yes," Virgil said.

"Good as you?"

"Probably not," Virgil said. "But there's a passel of them."

"You have a plan?" Stark said.

"Not yet," Virgil said.

"What do you think of Redmond's plan?" Stark said.

"They'll get slaughtered," Virgil said.

Stark nodded his head slowly, and kept nodding as he spoke.

"Yes," Stark said.

"You think we're afraid?" Redmond said.

Virgil looked at him and at me. I nodded.

"How many of your people have ever killed anybody?" I said.

"I don't know," Redmond said. "But we ain't backing down."

"Do you know anybody who ain't backing down who's ever killed anybody?" I said.

Redmond frowned at me. Then he shrugged.

"No," he said.

"Gunfight ain't like other things," Virgil said.

"Lujack's people are professionals," I said. "You'll get buried."

"He ain't gonna run us off," Redmond said.

Both fists were clenched in his lap. His face was red.

"Hell he ain't," Virgil said.

Redmond stood.

"You calling me a coward?" he said to Virgil.

Virgil looked at him as if he were an odd specimen of insect Virgil hadn't seen before.

"At the moment," Virgil said, "I'm calling you a fool."

"I'll fight you," Redmond said. "Goddamn it, I will."

"Bob," Stark said, "shut the fuck up."

"I ain't scared of him," Redmond said.

"Should be," Stark said, in a voice that would have cut through shale. "Now sit fucking down and shut fucking up. These people are trying to help you."

"We don't need it," Redmond said.

But he sat down.

"We could all go down, lumberjacks, us, everybody," he said. "There'd be like fifty of us."

"And leave who," I said, "looking out for the women and children?"

"They wouldn't . . ." Redmond said.

"'Course they would," Virgil said.

Redmond started to speak, and stopped and started again and stopped.

"Jesus," he said finally.

"Finally," Stark said to him, "do you get it? You know what you're dealing with?"

Redmond nodded silently.

"You'll help us," Stark said to Virgil.

"If you're going to stay with it," Virgil said. "If you ain't, me 'n Everett will ride off down to Texas."

"You'd run from Wolfson?" Redmond said.

"Got no reason not to," Virgil said. "'Less you folks are gonna stay and fight."

"We are," Redmond said softly. "We got no place else to go."

"Stark?" Virgil said.

"I'll be here," Stark said. "I'm not gonna ask my boys to go up against professional shooters. But there's enough of us, I think, to keep them out of here."

"Got enough food?" I said.

"For now," Stark said. "Shot an elk couple days ago. That'll help."

"Wolfson ain't gonna sell you none," I said.

"Nope."

"Any come in on the lumber train?"

Stark smiled without any amusement.

"Somebody blew the tracks of my spur about ten miles west of here," he said.

"So you can't sell your lumber, either," I said.

"Not for now."

Virgil looked at me.

"Well," he said. "Seems like we ought to clean this up pretty quick, Everett."

I nodded.

"What are you going to do?" Redmond said.

"We'll talk with Cato and Rose," Virgil said. "And you stay here and hold tight. Don't get caught out in the open."

"You four against twenty?" Stark said.

"At first," Virgil said.

# 62.

"What you suppose Wolfson's gonna do with all that sodbuster land he's got?" Rose said while we were eating breakfast in the Excelsior.

"Not much," I said, "because we ain't gonna let him keep it."

"Sure," Rose said. "But what's he think he's gonna do with it."

"Could run cattle," I said.

"Not the best range I ever seen," Rose said.

"Could reparcel it," I said. "Sell it off to a new crop of homesteaders."

"That's what he'll do," Virgil said. "Sell the land in house lots. The bank will hold the mortgages, so he'll still control it. They'll be new customers for the store and the saloons."

"So why not keep the sodbusters he's got now," Rose said.

"He's wrung 'em dry," Cato said.

All three of us looked at him. But he didn't add anything.

After a time Virgil said, "Cato's right. They got nothing. They can't repay a mortgage. They haven't got any money to spend at the emporium. They probably can't even rebuild enough to make a profit. But they can keep him from owning the land, and they can keep him from reselling to people who have some money."

"For him to squeeze out of the new folks," I said.

"So unless he can run them off, or starve them out, or kill them," Rose said, "these shitkickers are just in Wolfson's way."

"Yep."

"And they got nothing to bargain with," Rose said.

"Just us," I said.

Virgil appeared to be paying no attention to the conversation. He stood up suddenly.

"Think I'll go talk to Wolfson," he said, and walked out the front door of the saloon.

"What the fuck is he doing?" Rose said.

"Let's go see," I said.

We got up and went after Virgil.

Wolfson was at his table in the Blackfoot, and with him were Lujack and Swann.

"Virgil," Wolfson said, "I thought you'd be on your way to Texas by now."

Swann shifted a little in his chair. Virgil walked across the saloon and stopped in front of Wolfson.

"Used to work for you," Virgil said.

Wolfson nodded his head once.

"We ain't gonna let you run them settlers off their land," Virgil said.

No one at the table said anything for a long time. Virgil stood patiently. He was doing what he always did, just going about his business, plowing straight ahead. Nothing bothered him. He never seemed in a hurry, except things always seemed to happen faster for him than other people.

Finally, Wolfson said, "You're not?"

"Nope," Virgil said

"You and them three boys?" Lujack said, nodding at Cato and Rose and me.

"That's right," Virgil said. "Wanted to let you know. Give you a chance to negotiate, if you was of a mind to."

"Negotiate?" Lujack said.

Lujack was slowly discovering what so many people had discovered before him, that Virgil Cole was not like other folks.

"We ain't negotiating shit," Wolfson said. "You boys got a brain in your heads, you'll skedaddle the fuck out of Resolution while we're still willin' to let you."

Virgil nodded and looked at Swann.

"You got anything to say?" he said to him.

Swann looked lazily at Wolfson and Lujack seated with him, and then at me and Cato and Rose, behind Virgil.

"Not right now," he said.

They looked at each other. Swann didn't like the odds, and he was right. But he wasn't afraid of Virgil, which could be a mistake. Though as Virgil always insisted, you didn't know for certain until it happened.

Virgil nodded slowly.

Then, without speaking again, he turned and walked out of the saloon. Cato and Rose and I followed him.

# 63.

It'll be like it was with the Shoshones," I said. "They may not come, but you can't plan on it."

"We're losing manpower," Stark said, "every day. Mostly miners are moving on."

"Mine's dried up," Faison said. "Nothin' to hold 'em."

"Wolfson know that?" I said.

"They send somebody up every day to look at us," Stark said. "Coupla riders."

"Where?" I said.

"Top the ridge over there," Stark said.

He pointed west.

"Where we've cleared the trees," he said.

"When do they come?"

"Late afternoon."

"So the sun's behind them," Rose said.

"And anybody wanted to pick them off from down here," I said, "be shooting into it."

It was the middle of the afternoon. We were at the lumber camp, outside the lumber office, with Stark and Faison and Redmond and several men I didn't know. Virgil and Cato both looked up at the sun.

"Awful long shot, sun or no sun," I said.

"Better to be closer," Virgil said. "And not facing the sun."

Cato nodded and tapped himself on the chest. Virgil nodded back. Cato stood and walked away from the group and around the corner of the lumber office. Everyone watched him go. No one said anything.

So I said, after a time, "You need to stay careful. Keep your pickets posted on the road, and above the camp, too. Lujack and his posse may not come prancing up the road for you."

Stark and Faison nodded.

"So that's it?" Redmond said. "That's your plan? They're stealing our land and killing our people, and we sit here and wait for them to starve us out?"

Virgil looked at Redmond.

Since he never showed anything, only somebody who knew Virgil as well as I did would know how close Redmond was coming to the edge of Virgil's patience.

"That's what you should do," I said. "We got other plans."

"I want to know what they are," Redmond said. "I got a right. I got a right to know. I got a right to know where Tillson went. What's he doing? I . . ."

"Redmond," Virgil said.

His voice was so soft it was barely more than a whisper. But it was clear and hard, and all of us turned toward it. And Redmond stopped talking.

"You need to understand coupla things," Virgil said. "We got no quarrel with Wolfson. He hired us. He paid us, and when he didn't need us no more, he paid us off. Nothing wrong with any of that."

Redmond nodded.

"And we all need to make a living," Virgil said. "And there ain't one to be made here."

Virgil paused and looked around. No one said anything.

"And Everett and I need to get on down to Texas," Virgil said.

Redmond nodded.

"So we stayin' here is a big pain in the ass for us, and a big favor for you," Virgil said. "You got that part of it, Bob?"

Redmond nodded.

"Now, here's the other thing," Virgil said. "What we do, me, Everett, Cato, and Rose, what we do is a thing where you kind of feel your way along, extinctual, you might say."

"Instinctual," I said.

Virgil nodded approvingly.

"That's right. So people always askin' us what we gonna

do and how and when, we find that very annoying, especially when we doin' those people a big, large fucking favor for nothing."

Nobody said anything.

"You understand that?" Virgil said to Redmond.

"Yeah."

"Good. Then shut the fuck up and do what we tell you."

Redmond opened his mouth and couldn't seem to think of anything to say and shut it and nodded yes.

Virgil looked at him silently for another moment, then looked at me and nodded.

"So you got women and children here," I said. "And you got a lot of men with Winchesters, and nothing else to do. Put the men around the perimeter."

"Any advice on exactly where?" Stark said.

"You know the place better than I do," I said. "Just keep them close enough together so nobody can slide in between 'em. Change the guards often so they don't get skittish and shoot each other."

"Even though you don't think they'll come," Stark said.

"Ain't no reason for them to come," I said. "But people ain't always reasonable. And Wolfson's probably less reasonable than most."

"There's the riders," Rose said.

Squinting into the sun, I could see two horsemen on the top of the treeless hill. One might have had a telescope. As I watched, both of them whirled suddenly and reached for their guns. Before they cleared leather they toppled slowly from their horses, and the sound of two shots rolled down the hill toward us, slowed and softened by the distance.

"That'd be Cato," Rose said.

# 64.

Cato Tillson rode down the hill and into camp, hazing two riderless horses ahead of him.

"Figure it'll confuse 'em a little," Cato said, "if the horses don't come back."

"Spoils of war," Rose said.

Cato nodded and dismounted.

"You know how to take care of horses?" Virgil said to Redmond.

"'Course," Redmond said.

"Then take care of these," Virgil said.

Redmond looked sorta sullen about it, but he took the reins and led both horses off. The rest of the men drifted away. It was like Cato made them uneasy.

"Odds are improvin'," Virgil said. "You give them a chance."

"Yep," Cato said. "Called 'em out."

"What I hear," Virgil said, "that ain't much of a chance."

"It ain't," Cato said.

"Didn't expect it would be," Virgil said.

"There was two of 'em," Rose said.

"Ain't being critical," Virgil said, "just thinking about it."

"What's to think?" Rose said. "Cato's maybe the best I ever seen at this. He's supposed to slow down?"

"Nope."

"We're all good at this," Rose said. "Most fellas go up against any one of us in a fair fight, they ain't got much of a chance."

"So the fight ain't exactly fair anyway," Virgil said.

"No," I said. "It ain't. Never was."

Virgil nodded and walked a little distance away and looked silently into the woods. Redmond came back to the lumber office.

"How come you didn't bring them bodies down with you," Redmond said to Cato.

"Why?" Cato said.

Virgil turned when he heard Redmond.

"Them horses taken care of?" he said.

"Unsaddled 'em myself," Redmond said. "Fed 'em. Gave 'em water."

Virgil nodded.

"My older boy's currying them now," Redmond said.

Virgil nodded.

"Cato left them bodies up there," Virgil said, "so that by the time Lujack and his people found them, they'd be a mess."

"That ain't Christian," Redmond said.

"That's true," Virgil said. "But a body left out for the sun and the buzzards and such to work on it ain't a pretty thing to find. Lujack's posse might find it discouraging when they do."

"My God," Redmond said. "You people actually think like that."

Cato had gone into the office and gotten himself some coffee. He came out in time to hear Redmond's question, and he smiled faintly to himself and sat on the step and blew on the surface of the coffee, which was still too hot to drink. Virgil looked at me. I nodded and took a big breath and let it out.

"It ain't how we think," I said to Redmond. "It's how we are. You unnerstand? It's why we can do what we do. You ain't like that. Most people aren't. No reason to be. But we are, and what you need right now is people like us."

Redmond nodded.

"Yes," he said. "We do."

# 65.

It was a bright night, with a nearly full moon, when Cato and Rose, and me and Virgil, rode on down into Resolution. There wasn't much movement on the streets, but there was a lot of noise from the saloons. We rode in behind the Excelsior and turned into the passage that separated it from the laundry, and stopped. We sat our horses quietly in the shadows of the alley and waited.

"This ain't gonna work more'n once," I said.

"Once might be enough," Virgil said. "Make them come after us."

"And if it don't?" I said.

"We need to get them out in the open," Virgil said. "Can't fight them in here. Too many, still."

"So if this doesn't work," I said, "we find something else."

"We do," Virgil said.

Three men came out of the Excelsior and walked un-steadily down Main Street. They didn't see us.

"Thing is," I said, "if Wolfson wins this thing, he loses the town anyway."

"To?" Rose said.

"Lujack," I said. "Fella ain't a shooter hires twenty shoot-ers to work for him, and they're together long enough, what happens?"

Rose grinned dimly.

"Fella that ain't a shooter ends up working for the fellas that are," he said.

"Pretty much what happened with us," Virgil said. "Why Wolfson hired Lujack. He couldn't trust us to do what he said, and he couldn't make us."

"Not so much fun being Lujack," Rose said.

"He needs gunmen for what he wants," I said. "And he ain't one himself."

"Like a rabbit hiring coyotes," Rose said.

Two deputies came out of the hotel across the street.

"Making their rounds," Virgil murmured.

Frank Rose slid off his horse and handed the reins to Cato.

"Mine," he said. "Cato's two ahead of me."

Virgil nodded.

Rose stepped out into the street and walked behind the deputies. One of the deputies heard him and looked back, and said something to his partner. They both stopped and

turned. Rose stopped about forty feet away and stood looking at them. They didn't recognize him.

"You want something?" the deputy said.

"Kinda curious," Rose said, "'bout them Colts you're
carrying."

"Curious?" one of the deputies said.

"If you're any good with them," Rose said.

The two deputies moved away from each other, facing Rose

"Why you wantin' to know that?" the deputy said.

"'Cause I'm plannin' on shootin' you both," Rose said.
"'Less you're faster than me."

"You're what?" the deputy said.

"I was you I'd draw now, 'cause I'm fixin' to shoot,"
Rose said.

Rose drew. The deputies drew. Rose killed them both.
One shot each. Then he sprinted back to the alley where we
waited, took his reins back from Cato, and stepped up onto
his horse. Across the street, several deputies were easing out
of the hotel door, guns drawn.

"Sixteen to four," Rose said as he turned his horse.

"Every little bit helps," Virgil said.

And we wheeled and rode out of town at a full gallop.

# 66.

From where we sat, among some rocks at the top of the hill near the lumber camp, we could see the deputies out in force, posted at points around the town. In the late morning a squad of them, plus Lujack and Swann, rode halfway up the hill and, carefully out of rifle range, studied the area, riding in a slow arc in front of us. Lujack had a telescope.

"Got 'em frustrated," Virgil said.

I nodded. Virgil was leaning against the rocks. He straightened suddenly and turned. His Colt was in his hand. Beth Redmond came up the path behind us. The Colt was back in the holster. I doubt that she ever saw it.

"What are you looking at?" she said when she got to us.

"Our adversities," Virgil said.

"What?" she said.

"Our adversaries," I said.

"Oh."

Virgil nodded

"May I look?" she said.

"Surely," Virgil said.

Beth peeked over the top of one of the rocks.

"They're out of range," I said "You can just stand up and look, you want to."

She stood.

"Who is the one with the sort of Army hat on?" she said.

"Lujack," Virgil said. "One in the Stetson is named Swann. He's the shooting specialist."

"What are they doing?" she said.

"Trying to figure out a way to get to us," Virgil said.

"To kill you?"

"Yep."

She nodded, watching the riders as they moved slowly east to west, studying our situation.

"Do you think they'll attack us?" she said.

"Here?" Virgil said.

"Yes."

"Nope."

"Why not?"

"Too many men, with too much cover," Virgil said. "Lujack don't know the landscape, 'cept from a distance. He don't know what he'd ride into."

"So what are they doing?" she said.

"Trying to figure out something, just like us," Virgil said. "They've lost four men so far."

"Four men?"

"Yep."

"Cato Tillson shot a couple the other day, up on that hill," I said. "And Frank Rose killed a couple last night in Resolution."

"In Resolution?"

"Yep."

"That's so dangerous," she said. "What was he doing in there."

"We all went in," I said, "after dark, thought we might pick off one or two. Rose felt it was his turn."

"Why?"

"Why was it his turn?" I said.

"No, why did you all go in there."

"Trying to cut the odds," Virgil said.

He continued to watch the riders as he spoke.

"And trying to get them to come after us."

"Why do you want them to come after you?" she said.

"Get them out in the open," Virgil said. "See what we can do with them."

"They're out in the open now," she said, looking down at the riders.

"Not all of them," Virgil said.

"And they're too open," I said. "We'd have to cross a half-mile of open country to get to them. They are professional gunmen."

"So you wouldn't have a chance," Beth said.

"Not a big one," I said.

The deputies went out of sight around the curve of the hill.

"What if they sneak in behind you?" Beth said.

"Cato and Rose are up there," I said. "Other side of that hill. Between us, we can see the whole circle of the compass."

Beth looked up at the hill and then back down at the now-empty slope in front of us.

"Virgil," she said.

"'Course," Virgil said.

He was still watching the empty slope. I started to move away.

"No, stay, Everett," she said. "You can hear this."

I nodded and leaned back against the rock.

"My husband thinks you don't like him," Beth said to Virgil.

"I don't," Virgil said.

"Because of me?"

"Hard to like a man beats his woman," Virgil said.

"I know. God, don't I know that."

Virgil didn't say anything.

"But . . . Virgil, he's trying. He's trying so hard."

"Trying what?" Virgil said.

I could see Beth take in a big breath.

"He's trying so hard to be a man," she said. "He come from nothing, and he was still a boy when we come out here, and the land and the children were enough to break him, and . . . and now it's all plomped down on him: Indians, gunmen, killing. He's lost his land, he's trying to hold the other homesteaders together. . . . He's trying to hold himself together. . . . It's too much for him."

"He been hitting you again?" Virgil said.

"No, Virgil, he hasn't. I swear to God he hasn't touched me since I left him before the Indians."

"What would you like?" Virgil said.

"Don't treat him like a boy," she said. "Talk to him like he's a man."

Virgil stared at her for a long time without speaking.

"We meant something to each other," Beth said. "It wasn't just fucking. I know it wasn't."

"That's true," Virgil said.

"So please, Virgil, for me," she said. "Just treat him like a man."

Virgil nodded slowly.

"All right," he said.

# 67.

Virgil and I sat on our horses on the little rise that sloped down to what used to be the Redmond ranch. The burned-out buildings had been cleared, and the property was staked out in house lots that looked a good bit smaller than the original. Beyond where the house had stood was a creek that had cut its way maybe a foot deep into the prairie. A few cottonwoods grew along it.

"Cluster of trees there," Virgil said. "Provide some cover."

I nodded.

"Man and a horse, I'd say."

Virgil nodded, running his eyes over the layout.

"Hill over there, other side, beyond the house that way," he said.

"That would work, 'less they come that way."

"No reason they should," Virgil said.

"Might start getting cautious," I said. "We've picked off four of them so far."

Virgil shrugged.

"They do, the ball goes up a little sooner."

"Okay," I said.

"So," Virgil said. "We put two over there. One behind the cottonwoods."

He glanced around the hilltop where we were.

"One of us up here," he said, "back'a that outcroppin'."

"And Redmond down there, starting to rebuild," I said.

"Yep."

"You think he'll stay?" I said.

"Claims he will," Virgil said.

"But do you think so?" I said.

"Wants to be a man," Virgil said.

I didn't say anything.

"I ain't rubbin' Beth's nose in it," Virgil said. "If he can do it, it'll help us bed this thing down a lot earlier."

"And if he gets killed in the process?" I said.

"It's a risk you and me are taking," Virgil said. "And Cato and Rose, and we got a lot less at stake than he does."

"I know," I said.

We turned the horses and headed back toward the lumber camp, swinging wide around town as we went.

"Mrs. Redmond know about this plan?" I said.

"Don't know," Virgil said. "I didn't tell her."

"He will," I said.

"Maybe not," Virgil said. "Maybe scared he won't be able to carry it off, and don't want no one to know unless he does pull it off."

"You may be right," I said.

The horses were beginning to labor a little as we went uphill. We slowed them to a walk.

"When you want to do this?" I said.

"Tomorrow seems good," Virgil said.

"We go down early," I said.

"Three of us," Virgil said.

"And one of us brings Redmond down," I said. "Once we're in place."

"Be sure he comes," Virgil said. "I'd like you to do that."

"Sure," I said. "And if they see me with him?"

"Just one man," Virgil said.

He grinned.

"I know how fearsome you be, Everett," Virgil said. "But them deputies probably don't."

"Hope they spot him soon," I said. "I don't want to sit out here all day, or all week."

"We'll help them," Virgil said. "Have him build a cook fire, send up some smoke."

"You still didn't answer my question," I said. "Think he can do it?"

Virgil shook his head.

"Don't know," he said. "You."

"Don't know, either," I said.

Virgil grinned again.

"And he's our hole card," Virgil said.

# 68.

Virgil left with Cato and Rose before it was light. After sunup I went and collected Redmond. He had already hitched the wagon and loaded it with tools and lumber. He was carrying a Winchester. His face was pinched, and he looked pale. Mrs. Redmond was with him.

"Where are you going with my husband?" she said to me.

"Doing a little business," I said. "Shouldn't take long."

"He won't tell me where he's going," she said.

I nodded. Virgil had gotten that one right.

"Will you?" she said.

"No, ma'am," I said.

"Bob?" she said.

"Can't," he said.

He climbed into the wagon and stored the Winchester

under the wagon seat. He looked at his wife, and his children, who were staring at him wordlessly. I saw him swallow. Then he turned his head away and clucked at the mules and the wagon began to roll. I rode along beside it. I had my Colt on my hip, and a Winchester in a saddle scabbard under my left leg. Both weapons were .45s, so I could load both from my belt. I had the eight-gauge in a scabbard under my right leg, and a belt of shotgun shells looped over my saddle horn.

We didn't talk as we went, in a wide circle around Resolution, and on south downhill toward his land. Redmond was having trouble keeping his throat open. He swallowed often. He drank frequently from his canteen.

The lumber and tools rattled in the wagon bed. The harness creaked. The mules blew occasionally. Otherwise, no sound on the ride until we got to the top of the little hill where he could look down at the lots that had been marked out on the land where his house once stood. We stopped.

"Jesus," he said.

I nodded. He looked around.

"I don't see any of the others, Cole, those fellas."

"You're not supposed to," I said. "They're here."

"How do you know?" he said.

"They said they'd be here."

"Well, what if something happened? Can't they just let us know they're here?"

"And anyone that might have spotted us and is laying low with a spyglass?" I said.

"Well, could they maybe just whistle or something?"

"No," I said. "Now, you remember what we told you. Build a cook fire, send up some smoke. Park the wagon near where you're working. Leave the Winchester in it. If things start to happen, get behind the wagon. Take out the Winchester. Defend yourself."

He nodded painfully.

"Where you gonna go?" he said.

"I'm goin' downhill to the west, like I'm headin' on. Then I'm circlin' back in behind them cottonwoods along the creek."

"You really think somebody is watching us?" he said.

"Nope."

"But you're acting like they might be."

"Yep."

"'Cause you don't know they're not."

"Correct," I said. "Remember, stay close to the wagon. Trouble starts, get behind it."

"You scared, Everett," Redmond said.

"Of what? Dying? Fella asked Virgil Cole that question once, when we was marshalin' over in Appaloosa. Virgil says to him, 'You think me and Hitch are in this line of work 'cause we're scared to die?'"

"So you ain't?" Redmond said.

"Don't look forward to it, but no, I ain't scared enough so it gets in the way," I said.

"And Cole ain't scared."

"Hell, no," I said. "But, tell the truth, I don't think it really occurs to him that he might."

"I got a wife and kids," Redmond said.

"I know," I said. "That makes it harder."

I gestured toward the house lots at the foot of the hill. He slapped the reins and the mules started down.

"Don't forget to unhitch the mules," I said. "No reason they should get shot."

He nodded as he drove down the hill. I turned my horse and rode west like I said I would and when I was out of sight, looped back and came in behind the cottonwoods.

# 69.

It was probably the smoke from Redmond's fire that did it, but with the sun just a little west of noon, they came down the south side of one of the hills in the distance. Too far to be sure, but it looked like six of them riding two by two. They disappeared into the valley and came up over the next hill. They were six, a full squad of Lujack's deputies. Redmond saw them. He stood frozen for a moment, then looked furtively around.

*Don't look, goddamn it.*

The riders kept coming down into the next valley, out of sight, then reappearing on the top of our hill. They sat their horses for a moment, looking down at Redmond. The mules were unhitched, grazing toward the creek near my cottonwoods. Redmond stood frozen with a shovel in his hands in front of the wagon.

*Get behind the wagon.*

Redmond didn't move. He looked at the rifle under the wagon seat, then back at the riders.

*Behind the fucking wagon.*

The riders began to walk their horses down the last slope. I looked at the sky. The sun wasn't an issue. They were coming from the north. I was coming from the west, but the sun was so nearly straight up that it wasn't a factor. The riders came on. Close enough now so I could hear the sound of the horses' hooves on the dry surface of the prairie. Nobody had his gun out. These were essentially town men. Nobody was bent out of the saddle reading sign, seeing how many different horses had ridden by here. Probably weren't good at sign. And they were sure of themselves. They knew how to do this, and Redmond didn't. They'd probably spent a lifetime scaring clodhoppers.

*Behind the goddamned wagon.*

And suddenly Redmond moved. He turned and ran around the wagon as if his knees wouldn't bend. He looked again at the Winchester under the wagon seat. But he didn't touch it. Probably scared to start trouble.

The riders came to a halt in front of him and ranged out in a single row of six. One of them, probably the squad leader, spoke to Redmond.

"What are you doing?" he said.

Redmond stared at him for a moment. The squad leader

was tall and narrow, with sloping shoulders and a big hawk-ish nose.

"It's my land," he finally said.

Redmond's voice was hoarse.

"You think so," the squad leader said.

Redmond nodded. The squad leader took a big revolver out of his holster and held it easily by his side.

"What do you think," the squad leader said, "'bout being buried on it."

Redmond's voice was squeaky.

"I don't . . ." He started and didn't finish.

He looked at the cottonwoods, where he knew I was.

"Say good-bye to it, pig farmer," the squad leader said.

On the hill, Virgil Cole's horse stepped out from behind the rocks with Virgil sitting in the saddle. The horse stopped. Virgil drew and fired in the easy, liquid way he had and shot the squad leader between the shoulder blades. The squad leader pitched forward and draped over his horse's neck. The gun fell from his hand. The horse seemed disinterested. From behind the next hill down from Redmond, Cato and Rose came, pushing their horses hard, bent low over their horses' necks. I took out the eight-gauge and pushed my horse out of the trees, through the shallow stream, and came at the squad's right flank on a gallop. Virgil came somewhat more sedately down his hill and shot at least one more as he came. Redmond yanked the Winchester from under the wagon seat and dropped to the ground behind the wagon. I cut loose with the eight-gauge.

It is not easy to shoot from a moving horse. But if you're going to do it, an eight-gauge is the thing to do it with. The rider nearest me had his gun out and was turning toward me when the pellets hit him, about everywhere, and knocked him backward off his horse. The horse scrambled away from him as he fell, and then stopped and stood.

It was over very quick. Four of the deputies were on the ground by the time all of us reached the wagon. The other two were retreating at a gallop. One of the men on the ground was still moving in spasms. Cato rode over and from his horse shot the deputy in the head.

"Hate to see him suffer," Cato said.

"You want to ride the other two down?" Rose said.

The two runners were already over the second hill.

"Nope," Virgil said.

Redmond crawled out from under the wagon.

"I shot one," he said. "I think I shot one."

Virgil and I looked at each other.

"What?" Redmond said.

Virgil shook his head.

"Sort of ain't considered, ah, sportin'," Frank Rose said to him. "Counting up who shot who."

"Like counting your money," I said, "while you're playing poker."

"Why not?" Redmond said. "I don't get it."

Virgil looked at him briefly.

"No," Virgil said, "you don't."

He turned his horse and began to ride north toward the lumber camp. Redmond stared after him.

"He's just leavin'?" Redmond said. "Like that?"

Cato and Rose followed Virgil.

"Done what he came to do," I said. "Hitch them mules up."

"They're all leavin'," Redmond said.

"I rode out here with you," I said. "I'll ride back with you."

"But they musta heard the shooting in Resolution," Redmond said. "Won't they be riding out here?"

"Nope."

"Why not?"

"Take 'em a while to figure out it wasn't them shootin' you," I said. "And when they do, they'll stay where they are."

"Stay in town?"

"Yep."

"Why?"

"Odds are shrinking," I said. "They'll stay in town, protect themselves and Wolfson."

"They won't be coming after us?"

"Nope."

Redmond was harnessing the mules.

"Jesus Christ," he said. "It's like they ain't chasin' us. It's like now we're chasin' them."

"Sorta like that," I said.

# 70.

Frank Rose had liberated several bottles of whiskey from the Excelsior Saloon when he left. He and Cato and Virgil and I took one of them to our spot behind the rocks and passed it around.

"Redmond's down there telling anybody he can get to hold still," Rose said, "'bout the big battle out on his land."

"His first time," Virgil said.

"Think he actually fired that Winchester?" I said.

Nobody knew.

Above us the moon had waned into something a little more than half. There were a lot of stars, and we could see one another easily. I took some whiskey.

"So they're down there hunkered behind their fucking barricades," I said. "And we're up here hunkerin' behind ours."

"And running low on food," Rose said.

"Guess we got to go down and get them," Virgil said.

Cato nodded and reached for the bottle.

"Think we should," he said.

He drank, handed the bottle to Virgil, who drank.

"There's still twelve of 'em by my count," I said.

"Thirteen," Rose said, "if Wolfson will fight."

"Maybe we should keep sniping them off for a while longer," I said.

"Nope," Virgil said. "They ain't comin' out. And I wanna go to Texas."

"So we gotta go in," I said.

"Yep."

Nobody said anything. The bottle passed around some more. From the lumber camp we could hear an occasional domestic sound. Cook pot clattering. Children yelling.

"Think Redmond learned anything today?" I said.

"Nope," Virgil said.

"Think he can ever learn anything?" I said.

"Nope," Virgil said.

"Think he'll beat his wife again?"

"Maybe not," Virgil said.

The bottle came my way again. I took a drink.

"We can speak to him 'bout that 'fore we leave," I said.

"Yep," Virgil said.

He drank some whiskey and gave the bottle to Rose.

"There'll be sentries posted in town," I said.

"Sure there will," Virgil said.

"So we can't creep up on them so easy," Rose said.

"Nope."

We were quiet. The moon had moved west a little. The sounds from the lumber camp had died down. We heard an occasional night bird back in the woods, and somewhere below us and west a coyote was howling.

"They'll come to us," Virgil said.

Cato nodded.

"Why?" I said. "They sit tight and wait and after a while people will start drifting away. Not enough food, no way to earn a living, boredom, fear, they wait long enough we'll have nobody to protect, and in time Wolfson will get what he wants without shooting anybody."

"Two things," Virgil said. "Wolfson's stupid. He got no patience. Can't stand not getting what he wants. And this looks bad for Lujack. He can't drive off a bunch of sod-busters?"

"And us," I said.

"Four men," Virgil said. "Who's gonna hire him next time?"

"I wouldn't," I said.

"No," Virgil said. "You wouldn't. Also, he's an arrogant sonovabitch."

"He can't believe he can beat us," Rose said.

"Okay," I said. "I see that. So what do you think they'll do?"

"Don't know," Virgil said. "But they'll do something. All we got to do is be ready."

Rose leaned back against the rock. He looked up at the stars and took a pull at the whiskey bottle.

"Ain't got all that much else to do," he said.

# 71.

Three of us were playing cards for not much money behind the rocks. Cato was among the rocks, watching.

"Somebody coming," he said.

We all stood up and looked. A young woman was riding
an old fat gray roan up the open slope toward us. She didn't
look comfortable on the horse.

"Billie," I said.

"The little whore?" Virgil said.

"Yes."

Virgil nodded.

"Okay," he said. "It's a start. You talk to her, Everett. She
trusts you."

I waited until she was closer, then I walked out around
the stone outcropping and a little ways down the slope.

"Billie," I yelled.

She looked over.

"It's Everett," I said. "Ride over here."

She pulled the horse's head left, using both hands, and banged her small heels on the horse's ribs. I smiled. The horse lumbered slowly toward me.

"Nice to see you, Billie," I said when she arrived. "Everybody treating you good?"

"I'm all right, Everett," she said. "We miss you."

"I miss you, too," I said. "Where'd you get that horse?"

"Mr. Wolfson got it for me."

"And sent you up to talk with us?" I said.

"He gimme a note," Billie said.

She reached inside her dress and fumbled out a folded-up piece of paper and handed it to me.

"He says I should wait here for you to gimme an answer," Billie said.

"Can you hold the horse there okay?" I said.

Billie's skirts were hiked up to her thighs. Her legs were too short for the stirrups and stuck nearly straight out from the sides of the horse.

"I can ride a horse, Everett," Billie said.

"I can see that," I said. "You want to get off and sit, I'll boost you back up when it's time to go."

"I'm just fine right here," Billie said.

"Okay," I said. "I'll be back."

I went around the rocks and sat down and opened the paper and read it aloud.

*Virgil Cole,*

*I would like to meet with you and try to straighten out the trouble between us. Somewhere neutral, under a white flag. You can bring your men and I will bring mine. I'm sure we can work something out. Please tell Billie your answer.*

*Sincerely yours,*
*Amos Wolfson*

"Lemme see it," Virgil said.

I handed it to him, and he frowned over it as he read. Rose looked over his shoulder. Cato was still up in the rocks, watching.

"How's the girl doing out there," I said to Cato.

"Horse is eatin' grass," Cato said.

"She still got the reins?" I said.

"Yep."

Virgil handed the letter back to me.

"Whaddya think, Virgil?" Rose said.

Virgil shook his head and stood and walked around the rock and leaned on the downslope side of it and looked down at the town. He could see Billie, and Billie saw him. But he gave her no notice.

"What's he doing?" Rose said.

"He's thinking," I said.

"Hell," Rose said. "I never done enough of that to know it when I see it."

# 72.

From his side of the rocks, Virgil yelled to me.
"Come on out here," he said. "We'll talk to the girl."

I went out, and we walked over to Billie.

"Hello, Mr. Cole," Billie said.

Virgil tipped his hat.

"You take what I tell you back to Wolfson."

"He tole me you should write it down," Billie said.

"Ain't got a pencil," Virgil said. "I'll tell you simple. You'll remember."

Billie nodded.

"Tomorrow morning. An hour after sunup," Virgil said. "He brings Lujack and Swann with him. Nobody else.

They ride up here, stop out of rifle range. I'll see them and ride down."

"That's all?" Billie said.

"Say it back to me," Virgil said.

Billie repeated what Virgil had said.

"You'll remember it just that way," Virgil said.

"Yessir."

"Okay, Billie," Virgil said. "Ride on down and tell him."

"You're gonna meet them three by yourself," she said.

"I am," Virgil said. "Now go tell him."

"Yessir," Billie said.

She dragged the horse's head around and headed back down the hill. Virgil and I walked back in behind the rocks and sat down.

"You hear the plan?" I said to Cato and Rose.

"We could hear," Rose said.

"Wanna explain it to me a little?" I said to Virgil.

"I'm gonna kill 'em," he said.

"All three," I said.

"Yep."

"Alone," I said.

"Yep."

"Swann's a pretty fair gun hand," Rose said.

"So I hear," Virgil said.

"Why not bring us with you?" I said.

"'Cause they won't come," Virgil said. "Or they'll come with all their troops."

"True," I said.

"It's our chance," Virgil said, "to get them out in the open."

"You think they'll do it?" I said.

"They'll do it, long as it's three of them and just me," Virgil said.

"They'll have the rest of the outfit out of sight some-place," Rose said.

"Probably will," Virgil said. "But the closest cover is a fair piece. I figure I kill them and head up the hill, I'll be close enough for you to cover me before the rest can get there."

"They'll pull up," Cato said, "first one we knock down."

"And once they understand that it's over, they won't stick around," Virgil said.

"No," I said. "They won't. They got no stake in this."

"For crissake," Rose said. "They won't even be getting paid anymore."

"Swann wouldn't stick around," Virgil said, "Wolfson and Lujack were dead. But I gotta kill him first so's he won't get that chance."

"You pull this off," I said, "and we got the town."

"I don't," Virgil said, "and we're no worse off than we were."

"'Cept for you bein' dead," I said.

"'Cept for that," Virgil said.

# 73.

It was a bright, hot day. The sky was very high. And it was very still, with no wind, the stillness made more intense by the hum of insects. I watched the three riders come out of town and head toward the slope in front of us. They were walking their horses. No one was with them. At the foot of the slope they stopped.

"It's them," I said to Virgil. "Swann's on your right. West end of the line."

Virgil nodded and clucked to his horse and rode out around the stone outcropping, and started at a slow walk down the long slope. Through the glass, I scanned the area. No sign of deputies. If they were around, they were probably behind the higher ground to the east, where I couldn't see them. As Virgil rode down the slope, Cato and Rose lay in the rocks on either side of me with rifles. I had one, too, propped in the rocks in front of me while I was spy-glassing.

"You know what's making that sound?" Rose said. "I been hearing it all my life. I never seen the bug that makes it."

"I dunno," I said. "Locust, maybe?"

"Cicadas," Cato said.

Rose and I looked at each other.

"They make it with their hind legs," I said.

"What I heard," Rose said. "Rub 'em together."

"They make it with their belly," Cato said.

Rose and I nodded.

"See the funny-looking little bush there, where Virgil is now?" I said.

They did.

"I can hit that with a rifle," I said. "I tried it last night."

"I heard you," Cato said.

Must have been the excitement of the moment, for Cato, he was positively babbling.

"Okay," Rose said. "So if Virgil makes it back to there, he's in rifle range, and we can cover him."

It was long enough after sunrise so that there should have been activity in the lumber camp, but I didn't hear anything there, either. I don't know if the camp was laying low, holding its breath, or if I was just so locked on what was going on down the hill that I didn't hear anything. I noticed that the cicada sound no longer registered, either, so it probably had to do with concentrating.

"Virgil beats Swann," Cato said. "He may pull it off. I

don't know 'bout Lujack, but Wolfson pretty sure ain't much."

"Nobody, far as I know, ever beat Virgil," I said.

"If they had, he wouldn't be here," Rose said.

"True," I said.

"Swann's still here, too," Cato said.

"Also true," I said.

"So we'll see," Cato said.

"And pretty quick," I said.

Virgil reached the foot of the slope and stopped his horse maybe twenty feet in front of the three men. I looked at Swann through the glass. He was perfectly still on his horse, relaxed, looking at Virgil. Virgil had the same stillness in a fight. He had it now.

I put the glass away so I could see the whole scene.

Apparently, Wolfson said something and Virgil answered. Swann's gaze never wavered from Virgil. Then it seemed as if nobody said anything, as if everything stopped. Then, with no visible hurry, Virgil drew. Swann was good, he had cleared his holster when Virgil shot him and turned quietly and shot Lujack, as Lujack was still fumbling with his holster. Wolfson didn't draw. Instead, he raised both hands over his head as high as he could reach. Virgil shot him. There was almost a rhythm to it. As if something in Virgil's head was counting time. Swann. Lujack. Wolfson. Orderly. Graceful. One bullet each. And three men dead.

Then, with the three men on the ground and their rider-less horses starting to browse the short grass, Virgil opened the cylinder, took out the three spent shells, inserted three fresh ones, closed the cylinder, holstered his gun, turned his horse, and headed back up the hill at a dead gallop.

"Swann started things, 'stead of Virgil," Cato said, "he mighta won."

"But he didn't," I said.

# 74.

The deputies came boiling up over the hill where they figured to be, and rode hard after Virgil. There might have been ten. They were bunched, and at the distance and speed, it was hard to count for sure. When they came to the dead men, they reined in. Some of their horses were a little spooked about the corpses and shied and danced a little. Some didn't seem to notice that anything had happened. The horses of the dead men had paid very little attention, and were now eating grass a few feet from the bodies. I guess shooting bothered some horses and not others. Horses were hard to figure. Like people.

The deputies gathered, milling around the deceased as they discussed what to do. Nobody got down and checked on the dead men. They'd all seen it enough to recognize death when they saw it.

Virgil was well up the hill now, past the bush that marked rifle range. The deputies still milled. Virgil's horse pounded up to the rock outcropping and around it. His hooves clattered where some of the ledge was exposed underfoot, and then he was behind the rocks, breathing in big huffs. Virgil slid off him, took a loop around a tree with the reins, and joined us in the rocks.

"Swann was good," Virgil said

Below us, the deputy with the big mustache, who had killed three men in Ellsworth, rode a ways up the hill but stopped a long way short of the rifle-range bush.

"Cole," he shouted.

Virgil climbed down from the rocks and went out in front of them, and stood. I slid forward a little so I could see him.

"You hear me, Cole?" the deputy shouted.

"Yep."

"We got no stake in this, we're hired hands. For us, the job's over."

Virgil waited.

"You hear that?" the deputy yelled.

"Yep."

"We'll be out of here by tomorrow night," the deputy shouted.

Virgil didn't say anything for a minute. He looked up at me looking down from the rocks, and he grinned.

Then he turned back to the deputy down the slope and waved his right hand.

"*Hasta la vista,*" he shouted.

And the deputy turned his horse and headed back down the slope and joined the other deputies. They left the bodies where they had lain, rounded up the riderless horses, and drove them ahead of them as they went back into town. After maybe an hour or so, someone came from town in a buckboard and gathered up the bodies.

# 75.

We had a pack mule for supplies, and were saying good-bye to Cato and Rose, when Beth Redmond came out of the hotel that used to belong to Wolfson.

"You're really going," she said.

"Yes, ma'am," I said.

"I'll miss you."

"We'll miss you, too, ma'am," I said. "Won't we, Virgil."

"We will," Virgil said.

"You know, the men got together and elected Mr. Stark mayor of Resolution," she said.

"Yep," Virgil said.

"He's going to run the bank and the store and everything that poor Mr. Wolfson, ah, left behind."

"Stark knows how to run things," I said.

"Everybody wanted both of you to stay on, too," she said.

"These boys'll make a fine pair of marshals," Virgil said.

Rose grinned at her.

"Like my new badge?" he said.

"You and Mr. Tillson look very nice," she said.

No one mentioned that the badges were lifted from the dead bodies of Lujack and Swann.

"You have any problems," Virgil said, "with anybody, you understand? You see Cato or Rose, they'll straighten it out."

She nodded.

"Will you be coming back this way anytime?" she said.

"Never know," Virgil said. "Right now I got to go to Texas."

She stood in front of him, looking at him for a moment, then she put her arms around him and kissed him hard on the mouth.

"You're a good man, Virgil Cole," she said when she was through. "Thank you."

Virgil grinned at her.

"You're welcome," he said, and patted her on the backside, and swung up onto his horse.

She gave me a little hug, too, and a kiss on the cheek, but with less enthusiasm. I hugged her back gently.

"Good-bye, Beth," I said, and got on the horse.

Virgil looked down at Beth.

"Remember, he gives you any trouble . . ."

"Come see us," Rose said.

"He's changed," Beth said. "But thank you."

Beth turned and went back into the hotel. Virgil and I looked at Cato and Rose.

"Never got to fight you," Virgil said.

"Not this time," Rose said.

"Probably just as well," Virgil said.

"Probably," Cato said.

We nodded. They nodded. Then we started the horses and headed south out of Resolution.

Virgil didn't say anything the whole day. We were in open country when we camped that night. I took a bottle of whiskey out of my saddlebag, and we had some while we made a fire and cooked some sowbelly and beans under the big, dark sky.

"You think he'll leave her alone?" Virgil said.

"Redmond?" I said. "Probably not."

"Be all right for a while," Virgil said. "Then something'll go wrong and he'll be under pressure. . . ."

"And he won't be man enough to handle it," I said. "So he'll convince himself it's her fault and smack her couple times to make himself feel better."

"He hurts her," Virgil said, "Cato will kill him."

"I know," I said.

"And it'll break her heart," he said.

"Yep."

"But she'll be better off," Virgil said.

"She won't think so for a while," I said.

Virgil leaned back against his saddle and drank from the bottle and looked up at the infinite scatter of stars.

"She was a nice clean woman," he said. "Always took a bath 'fore we done anything."

I didn't comment. He handed me the bottle. I had some.

"Smart," he said. "Good lookin', good hearted. Hard to figure why she'd love a jackass like Redmond."

I said, "Uh-huh."

"But she does," Virgil said.

"Uh-huh."

Virgil took another turn on the bottle, then he looked at me and grinned.

"She's such a dope," he said. "He ran off to Texas with somebody else, she'd go on down there looking for him."

"Uh-huh," I said.

I put my hand out for the bottle and Virgil passed it to me.

"And her friend would go with her," he said.

I drank some whiskey.

"Uh-huh," I said.